VOLUME 1

Edited by **Jeff Conner**

Illustrated by **Mike Dubisch**

Cover painting by **Menton3**

SAN DIEGO, CA
2011

Book Design by Robbie Robbins

www.IDWPUBLISHING.com

ISBN: 978-1-60010-962-1

14 13 12 11   1 2 3 4

Become our fan on Facebook **facebook.com/idwpublishing** • Follow us on Twitter **@idwpublishing** • Check us out on YouTube **youtube.com/idwpublishing**

Ted Adams, CEO & Publisher • Greg Goldstein, Chief Operating Officer • Robbie Robbins, EVP/Sr. Graphic Artist
Chris Ryall, Chief Creative Officer/Editor-in-Chief • Matthew Ruzicka, CPA, Chief Financial Officer • Alan Payne, VP of Sales

REQUIRED READING REMIX, VOLUME 1. JUNE 2011. FIRST PRINTING. Required Reading Remix © 2011 Idea and Design Works, LLC. All Rights
Reserved. Cover painting copyright © 2011 by Menton J. Mathews III. Illustrations copyright © 2011 by Mike Dubisch. All stories copyright © 2011 by
their respective authors. IDW Publishing, a division of Idea and Design Works, LLC. Editorial offices: 5080 Santa Fe St., San Diego, CA 92109. Any
similarities to persons living or dead are purely coincidental. With the exception of artwork and/or brief text excerpts used for review purposes, none of
the contents of this publication may be reprinted without the permission of Idea and Design Works, LLC. Printed in Korea.
IDW Publishing does not read or accept unsolicited submissions of ideas, stories, or artwork.
Originally published as part of *Classics Mutilated*.

Table of Contents

🍂 🍂

REQUIRED READING REMIXED

Dread Island

By

Joe R. Lansdale

This here story is a good'n, and just about every word of it is true. It's tempting to just jump to the part about where we seen them horrible things, and heads was pulled off and we was in a flying machine and such. But I ain't gonna do it, 'cause Jim says that ain't the way to tell a proper yarn.

Anyhow, this here story is as true as that other story that was written down about me and Jim. But that fella wrote it down made all the money and didn't give me or Jim one plug nickel of it. So, I'm going to try and tell this one myself like it happened, and have someone other than that old fart write it down for me, take out most of the swear words and such, and give you a gussied up version that I can sell and get some money.

Jim says when you do a thing like that, trying to make more of something than it is, it's like you're taking a drunk in rags and putting a hat on him and giving him new shoes with ties in them, and telling everybody he's from up town and has solid habits. But anyone looks at him, they're still gonna see the rags he's wearing and know he's a drunk 'cause of the stagger and the smell. Still, lots of drunks are more interesting than bankers, and they got good stories, even if you got to stand downwind to hear them in comfort.

If I get somebody to write it down for me, or I take a crack at it, is yet to be seen. All I know right now is it's me talking and you listening, and you can believe me or not, because it's a free country. Well, almost a free country, unless your skin ain't white. I've said it before: I know it ain't right in the eyes of God to be friends with a slave, or in Jim's case, an ex-slave that's got his free papers. But even if it ain't right, I don't care. Jim may be colored, but he has sure fire done more for me than God. I tried praying maybe a dozen times, and the only thing I ever got out of it was some sore knees. So, if I go to hell, I go to hell.

Truth is, I figure heaven is probably filled with dogs, 'cause if you get right down to it, they're the only ones deserve to be there. I don't figure a cat or a lawyer has any chance at all.

Anyway, I got a story to tell, and keep in mind—and this part is important— I'm trying to tell mostly the truth.

Now, any old steamboater will tell you, that come the full moon, there's an is- land out there in the wide part of the Mississippi. You're standing on shore, it's so far out it ain't easy to see. But if the weather's just right, and you got some kind of eye on you, you can see it. It don't last but a night—the first night of the full moon—and then it's gone until next time.

Steamboats try not to go by it, 'cause when it's there, it has a current that'll drag a boat in just like a fella with a good stout line pulling in a fish. I got word about it from half a dozen fellas that knew a fella that knew a fella that had boated past it and been tugged by them currents. They said it was all they could do to get away. And there's plenty they say didn't get away, and ain't never been heard of again.

Another time, me and Tom Sawyer heard a story about how sometimes you could see fires on the island. Another fella, who might have been borrowing the story from someone else, said he was out fishing with a buddy, and come close to the island, and seen a post go up near the shore, and a thing that wasn't no kind of man was fastened to it. He said it could scream real loud, and that it made the hairs on the back of his neck stand up. He said there was other things dancing all around the post, carrying torches and making a noise like yelling or some such. Then the currents started pulling him in, and he had to not pay it any more mind, because he and his buddy had to row for all they was worth to keep from being sucked onto the island.

When we got through hearing the story, first thing Tom said was, "Someday, when the moon is right, and that island is there, I'm gonna take a gun and a big Bowie knife, and I'm going to go out there. I'll probably also have to pack a lunch."

That danged old island is called Dread Island, and it's always been called that. I don't know where it got that name, but it was a right good one. I found that out because of Tom and Joe.

Way this all come about, was me and Jim was down on the bank of the river, night fishing for catfish. Jim said there was some folks fished them holes by sticking their arms down in them so a catfish would bite. It wasn't a big bite, he said, but they clamped on good and you could pull them out that way, with them hanging on your arm. Then you could bust them in the head, and you had you something good to eat. He also said he wouldn't do that for nothing. The idea of sticking his hand down in them holes bothered him to no end, and just me thinking on it didn't do me no good either. I figured a gator or a moccasin snake was just as likely to bite me, and a fishing line with a hook on it would do me just as good. Thinking back on that, considering I wouldn't put my hand in a hole for fear something might bite it, and then me going out to Dread Island, just goes to show you can talk common sense a lot more than you can act on it.

But anyway, that ain't how this story starts. It starts like this.

So, there we was, with stinky bait, trying to catch us a catfish, when I seen Becky Thatcher coming along the shoreline in the moonlight.

Now Becky is quite a nice looker, and not a bad sort for a girl; a breed I figure is just a step up from cats. Jim says my thinking that way is because I'm still young and don't understand women's ways. He also explained to me their ways ain't actually understandable, but they sure do get a whole lot more interesting as time goes on.

I will say this. As I seen her coming, her hair hanging, and her legs working under that dress, the moonlight on her face, I thought maybe if she wasn't Tom's girl, I could like her a lot. I'm a little ashamed to admit that, but there you have it.

Anyway, she come along, and when she saw us, she said, "Huck. Jim. Is that you?"

I said, "Well, if it ain't, someone looks a whole lot like us is talking to you."

She come over real swift like then. She said, "I been looking all over for you. I figured you'd be here."

"Well," I said, "we're pretty near always around somewhere or another on the river."

"I was afraid you'd be out on your raft," she said.

"We don't like to go out on the water the night Dread Island is out there," I said.

She looked out over the water, said, "I can't see a thing."

"It looks just like a brown line on top of the water, but it's sharp enough there in the moonlight," I said. "If you give a good look."

"Can you see it too, Jim?" she asked.

"No, Miss Becky, I ain't got the eyes Huck's got."

"The island is why I'm looking for you," she said. "Tom has gone out there with Joe. He's been building his courage for a long time, and tonight, he got worked up about it. I think maybe they had some liquid courage. I went to see Tom, and he and Joe were loading a pail full of dinner into the boat. Some cornbread and the like, and they were just about to push off. When I asked what they were doing, Tom told me they were finally going to see Dread Island and learn what was on it. I didn't know if he was serious. I'm not even sure there is an island, but you tell me you can see it, and well ... I'm scared he wasn't just talking, and really did go."

"Did Tom have a big knife with him?" I asked.

"He had a big one in a scabbard stuck in his belt," she said. "And a pistol."

"What do you think, Jim?" I asked.

"I think he's done gone out there, Huck," Jim said. "He said he was gonna, and now he's got that knife and gun and dinner. I think he's done it."

She reached out and touched my arm and a shock run through me like I'd been struck by lightning. It hurt and felt good at the same time, and for a moment there, I thought I'd go to my knees.

"Oh, my God," she said. "Will they be all right?"

"I reckon Tom and Joe will come back all right," I said, but I wasn't really that sure.

She shook her head. "I'm not so certain. Could you and Jim go take a look?"

"Go to Dread Island?" Jim said. "Now, Miss Becky, that ain't smart."

"Tom and Joe went," she said.

"Yes, ma'am," Jim said, like she was a grown woman, "and that proves what I'm saying. It ain't smart."

"When did they go?" I said.

"It was just at dark," she said. "I saw them then, and they were getting in the boat. I tried to talk Tom out of it, because I thought he was a little drunk and shouldn't be on the water, but they went out anyway, and they haven't come back."

I figured a moment. Nightfall was about three or four hours ago.

I said, "Jim, how long you reckon it takes to reach that island?"

"Couple of hours," Jim said, "or something mighty close to that."

"And a couple back," I said. "So what say we walk over to where Tom launched his boat and take a look. See if they done come in. They ain't, me and Jim will go take a gander for him."

"We will?" Jim said.

I ignored him.

Me and Jim put our lines in the water before we left, and figured on checking them later. We went with Becky to where Tom and Joe had pushed off in their boat. It was a pretty far piece. They hadn't come back, and when we looked out over the water, we didn't see them coming neither.

Becky said, "Huck, I think I see it. The island, I mean."

"Yeah," I said, "there's a better look from here."

"It's just that line almost even with the water, isn't it?" she said.

"Yep, that's it."

"I don't see nothing," Jim said. "And I don't want to."

"You will go look for him?" Becky said.

"We'll go," I said.

"We will?" Jim said again.

"Or I can go by myself," I said. "Either way."

"Huck," Jim said, "you ought not go out there. You ain't got no idea what's on that island. I do. I heard more stories than you have, and most of it's way worse than an entire afternoon in church and having to talk to the preacher personal like."

"Then it's bad," I said, and I think it was pretty obvious to Becky that I was reconsidering.

Becky took my arm. She pulled herself close. "Please, Huck. There's no one else to ask. He's your friend. And then there's Joe."

"Yeah, well, Joe, he's sort of got his own look-out far as I'm concerned," I said. I admit I said this 'cause I don't care for Joe Harvey much. I ain't got no closer friend than Jim, but me and Tom was friends too, and I didn't like that he'd asked Joe to go with him out there to Dread Island and not me. I probably wouldn't have gone, but a fella likes to be asked.

"Please, Huck," she said, and now she was so close to me I could smell her, and it was a good smell. Not a stink, mind you, but sweet like strawberries. Even there in the moonlight, her plump, wet lips made me want to kiss them, and I had an urge to reach out and stroke her hair. That was something I wasn't altogether understanding, and it made me feel like I was coming down sick.

Jim looked at me, said, "Ah, hell."

Our raft was back where we had been fishing, so I told Becky to go on home and I'd go look for Tom and Joe, and if I found them, I'd come back and let her know or send Tom to tell her, if he hadn't been ate up by alligators or carried off by mermaids. Not that I believed in mermaids, but there was them said they was out there in the river. But you can't believe every tall tale you hear.

All the while we're walking back to the raft, Jim is trying to talk me out of it.

"Huck, that island is all covered in badness."

"How would you know? You ain't never been. I mean, I've heard stories, but far as I know, they're just stories."

I was talking like that to build up my courage; tell the truth, I wasn't so sure they was just tall tales.

Jim shook his head. "I ain't got to have been. I know someone that's been there for sure. I know more than one."

I stopped walking. It was like I had been stunned with an ox hammer. Sure, me and Tom had heard a fella say he had been there, but when something come from Jim, it wasn't usually a lie, which isn't something I can say for most folks.

"You ain't never said nothing before about that, so why now?" I said. "I ain't saying you're making it up 'cause you don't want to go. I ain't saying that. But I'm saying why tell me now? We could have conversated on it before, but now you tell me."

Jim grabbed my elbow, shook me a little, said, "Listen here, Huck. I ain't never mentioned it before because if someone tells you that you ought not to do something, then you'll do it. It's a weakness, son. It is."

I was startled. Jim hadn't never called me son before, and he hadn't never mentioned my weakness. It was a weakness me and Tom shared, and it wasn't something I thought about, and most of the time I just figured I did stuff 'cause I wanted to. But with Jim saying that, and grabbing my arm, calling me son, it just come all over me of a sudden that he was right. Down deep, I knew I had been thinking about going to that island for a long time, and tonight just set me a purpose. It was what them preachers call a revelation.

"Ain't nobody goes over there in they right mind, Huck," Jim said. "That ole island is all full of haints, they say. And then there's the Brer People."

"Brer People," I says. "What in hell is that?"

"You ain't heard nothing about the Brer people? Why I know I ain't told you all I know, but it surprises me deep as the river that you ain't at least heard of the Brer people. They done come on this land from time to time and do things, and then go back. Them fellas I know been over there and come back, both of them colored, they ain't been right in they heads since. One of them lost a whole arm, and the other one, he lost his mind, which I figure is some worse than an arm."

"You sure it's because they went out to Dread Island?"

"Well, they didn't go to Nantucket," Jim said, like he had some idea where that was, but I knew he didn't. It was just a name he heard and locked onto.

"I don't know neither them to be liars," Jim said, "and the one didn't lose his senses said the Brer People was out there, and they was lucky to get away. Said the island was fading when they got back to their boat. When it went away, it darn near pulled them after it. Said it was like a big ole twister on the water, and then it went up in the sky and was gone."

"A twister?"

"What they said."

I considered a moment. "I guess Brer People or not, I got to go."

"You worried about that Miss Becky," Jim said, "and what she thinks?"

"I don't want her upset."

"I believe that. But you thinking you and her might be together. I know that's what you thinking, 'cause that's what any young, red-blooded, white boy be thinking about Miss Becky. I hope you understand now, I ain't crossing no color lines in my talk here, I'm just talking to a friend."

"Hell, I know that," I said. "And I don't care about color lines. I done decided if I go to hell for not caring about that, at least you and me will be there to talk. I figure too that danged ole writer cheated us out of some money will be there too."

"Yeah, he done us bad, didn't he?"

"Yeah, but what are these Brer People?"

We had started walking again, and as we did, Jim talked.

"Uncle Remus used to tell about them. He's gone now. Buried for some twenty years, I s'pect. He was a slave. A good man. He knew things ain't nobody had an inkling about. He come from Africa, Huck. He was a kind of preacher man, but the gods he knew, they wasn't no god of the Bible. It wasn't no Jesus he talked about, until later when he had to talk about Jesus, 'cause the massas would beat his ass if he didn't. But he knew about them hoodoo things. Them animals that walked like men. He told about them even to the whites, but he made like they was little stories. I heard them tales when I was a boy, and he told them to me and all the colored folks in a different way."

"You ain't makin' a damn bit of sense, Jim."

"There's places where they show up. Holes in the sky, Uncle Remus used to say. They come out of them, and they got them some places where they got to stay when they come out of them holes. They can wander some, but they got to get back to their spot a'fore their time runs out. They got 'strictions. That island, it's got the same 'strictions."

"What's ''strictions'?"

"Ain't exactly sure, but I've heard it said. I think it means there's rules of a sort."

By this time we had come to the raft and our fishing lines, which we checked right away. Jim's had a big ole catfish on it.

Jim said, "Well, if we gonna go to that dadburn island, we might as well go with full bellies. Let's get out our gear and fry these fish up."

"You're going then?" I said.

Jim sighed. "I can't let you go out there by yourself. Not to Dread Island. I did something like that I couldn't sleep at night. "Course, I didn't go, I would at least be around to be without some sleep."

"Go or don't go, Jim, but I got to. Tom is my friend, and Becky asked me. If it was you, I'd go."

"Now, Huck, don't be trying to make me feel bad. I done said I'd go."

"Good then."

Jim paused and looked out over the river.

"I still don't see it," Jim said, "and I'm hoping you just think you do."

We cooked up those catfish and ate them. When we was done eating, Jim got his magic hairball out of the ditty bag he carried on a rope around his waist. He took a gander at it, trying to divine things. That hairball come from the inside of a cow's stomach, and Jim said it had more mystery in it than women, but was a lot less good to look at. He figured he could see the future in it, and held stock by it.

Jim stuck his big thumbs in it and moved the hair around and eyeballed it some, said, "It don't look good, Huck."

"What's that hairball telling you?" I was looking at it, but I didn't see nothing but a big ole wad of hair that the cow had licked off its self and left in its stomach before it got killed and eat up; it smelled like an armpit after a hard day of field work.

Jim pawed around some more, then I seen his face change.

He said, "We go out there, Huck, someone's gonna die."

"You ain't just saying that about dying 'cause you don't want to go, are you?" I said.

He shook his head. "I'm saying it, 'cause that's what the hairball says."

I thought on that a moment, then said, "But that don't mean it's me or you dying, does it?"

Jim shook his head again. "No. But there ain't no solid way of telling."

"It's a chance we have to take," I said.

Jim stood for a moment just looking at me, shoving that hairball back into his pants pocket.

"All right," he said. "If that's how it is, then put this in your left shoe."

He had whittled a little cross, and it was small enough I could slide it down the side of my shoe and let it press up against the edge of my foot. Jim put a cross in his shoe too. We didn't normally have no shoes, but some good Samaritans gave them to us, and we had taken to wearing them now and again. Jim said it was a sure sign we was getting civilized, and the idea of it scared me to death. Civilizing someone meant they had to go to jobs; and there was a time to show up and a time to leave; and you had to do work in between the coming and leaving. It was a horrible thing to think about, yet there I was with shoes on. The first step toward civilization and not having no fun anymore.

I said, "Is that cross so Jesus will watch over us?"

"A cross has got them four ends to it that show the four things make up this world. Fire, wind, earth, and water. It don't do nothing against a regular man, but against raw evil, it's supposed to have a mighty big power."

"But you don't know for sure?" I said.

"No, Huck, I don't. They're ain't much I know for sure. But I got these too."

Jim held up two strings, and each of them had a big nail tied to it.

"These supposed to be full of power against evil," he said.

"Ain't the nails on account of Jesus?" I said. "Them being stuck in his hands and feet and such. I think I was told that in Sunday school. It's something like a cymbal."

"A cymbal? Like you hit in a band?"

"You know, I ain't sure, but I think that's what I was told."

"I don't see it being about no cymbals," Jim said. "Iron's got magic in it, that's all I know. It had magic in it before anyone ever heard of any Jesus. It's just iron to us, but to them haints, well, it's a whole nuther matter. Here. Loop this here string over your neck and tie the other end back to the nail. Make you a necklace of it. That ought to give you some protection. And I got some salt here in little bags for us. You never know when you might have the devil on your left, which is where he likes to stay, and if you feel him there, you can toss salt over your left shoulder, right into his eye. And we can use some of it on something to eat, if we got it."

"Finally," I said, "something that sounds reasonable."

When I had the nail around my neck, the cross in my shoe, and the bag of salt in my pocket, and my pocketknife shoved down tight in my back pocket, we pushed off the raft. Moment later we was sailing out across the black night water toward Dread Island.

The water was smooth at first, and the long pushing poles helped us get out in the deep part. When we got out there, we switched to Jim using the tiller, and me handling the sails, which is something we had added as of recent. They worked mighty good, if you didn't shift wrong; and, of course, there had to be wind.

It had been pretty still when we started out, and that had worried me, but before long, a light wind come up. It was just right, filling that canvas and pushing us along.

It didn't seem long before that line of dark in the water was a rise of dark, and then it was sure enough an island. Long and low and covered in fog, thick as the wool on a sheep's ass.

The raft started moving swift on account of it was caught up in a current, and before we knowed it, we was going through the fog and slamming up on the bank of Dread Island. We got out and used the docking rope to drag the raft on shore. It was a heavy rascal out of the water, and I thought I was gonna bust a gut. But we finally got it pulled up on solid ground.

Right then, there wasn't much to see that was worth seeing. The fog was heavy, but it was mostly around the island. On the island itself it was thin. Off to my right, I could see briars rising up about ten feet high, with dark thorns on them bigger than that nail I had tied around my neck. The tips of them were shiny in the moonlight, and the bit of fog that was off the water, twisted in between them like stripped wads of cotton. To the left, and in front of us, was some woods; it was as dark in there as the inside of a dog's gut.

"Well, here we is all ready for a rescue," Jim said. "And we don't even know they here anywhere. They may have done come and gone home. They could have come back while we was frying catfish and I was looking at my hairball."

I pointed to the mud gleaming in the moonlight, showed Jim there was a drag line in it.

"That looks like the bottom of a boat," I said.

Jim squatted down and touched the ground with his fingers. "It sure do, Huck."

We followed the drag line until we come to a patch of limbs. I moved them back, and seen they had been cut and was thrown over the boat to hide it.

"I figure this is their boat," I said. "They're exploring, Jim. They done hid the boat, and gone out there."

"Well, they didn't hide it so good," he said, "'cause it took us about the time it takes a duck to eat a June bug to find it."

We got a big cane knife off the raft, and Jim took that and cut down some limbs, and we covered the raft up with them. It wasn't a better hiding place than Tom and Joe's boat, but it made me feel better to do it.

With Jim carrying the cane knife, and me with a lit lantern, we looked for sign of Tom and Joe. Finally, we seen some footprints on the ground. One was bare-foot, and the other had on shoes. I figured Tom, who had been getting civilized too, would be the shoe wearer, and Joe would be the bare footer.

Their sign led off in the woods. We followed in there after them. There was hardly any moon now, and even with me holding the lantern close to the ground, it wasn't no time at all until we lost track of them.

We kept going, and after a while we seen a big old clock on the ground. I held the lantern closer, seen it was inside a skeleton. The skeleton looked like it be-longed to an alligator. Inside them alligator bones was human bones, all broke up, along with what was left of a hat with a feather in it, a boot, and a hook of the sort fits on a fella with his hand chopped off.

It didn't make no sense, but I quit thinking about, because I seen something move up ahead of us.

I wasn't sure what I had seen, but I can tell you this, it didn't take but that little bit of a glance for me to know I didn't like the looks of it.

Jim said, "Holy dog turd, was that a man with a rabbit's head?"

I was glad he said that. I had seen the same darn shadowy thing, but was think-ing my mind was making it up.

Then we saw movement again, and that thing poked its head out from behind a tree. You could see the ears standing up in the shadows. I could see some big white buckteeth too.

Jim called out, "You better come out from behind that tree, and show yourself good, or I'm gonna chop your big-eared head off with this cane knife."

That didn't bring the thing out, but it did make it run. It tore off through them woods and underbrush like its tail was on fire. And it actually had a tail. A big cotton puff that I got a good look at, sticking out of the back of a pair of pants.

I didn't figure we ought to go after it. Our reason for being here was to find Tom and Joe and get ourselves back before the light come up. Besides, even if that thing was running, that didn't give me an idea about chasing it down. I might not like it if I caught it.

So, we was standing there, trying to figure if we was gonna shit or go blind, and that's when we heard a whipping sound in the brush. Then we seen torches. It didn't take no Daniel Boone to figure that it was someone beating the bushes, driving game in front of it. I reckoned the game would be none other than that thing we saw, so I grabbed Jim's arm and tugged him back be-hind some trees, and I blowed out the light. We laid down on our bellies and watched as the torches got closer, and they was bright enough we could see what was carrying them.

Their shadows come first, flickering in the torchlight. They was shaped something odd, and the way they fell on the ground, and bent around trees, made my skin crawl. But the shadows wasn't nothing compared to what made them.

Up front, carrying a torch, was a short fella wearing blue pants with rivets up the side, and he didn't have on no shirt. His chest was covered in a red fur and he had some kind of pack strapped to his back. His head, well, it wasn't no human head at all. It was the head of a fox. He was wearing a little folded hat with a feather in it. Not that he really needed that feather to get our attention. The fact that he was walking on his hind paws, with shoes on his feet, was plenty enough.

With him was a huge bear, also on hind legs, and wearing red pants that come to the knees. He didn't have no shoes on, but like the fox, he wasn't without a hat. Had a big straw one like Tom Sawyer liked to wear. In his teeth was a long piece of some kind of weed or another. He was working it from one side of his mouth to the other. He was carrying a torch.

The other four was clearly weasels, only bigger than any weasels I had ever seen. They didn't have no pants on at all, nor shoes neither, but they was wearing some wool caps. Two of the weasels had torches, but the other two had long switch limbs they was using to beat the brush.

But the thing that made me want to jump up and grab Jim and run back toward the raft, was this big nasty shape of a thing that was with them. It was black as sin. The torch it was carrying flickered over its body and made it shine like fresh licked licorice. It looked like a big baby, if a baby could be six foot tall and four foot wide. It was fat in the belly and legs. It waddled from side to side on flat, sticky feet that was picking up leaves and pine needles and dirt. It didn't have no real face or body; all of it was made out of that sticky black mess. After awhile, it spit a stream that hit in the bushes heavy as a cow pissing on a flat rock. That stream of spit didn't miss me and Jim by more than ten feet. Worse, that thing turned its head in our direction to do the spitting, and when it did, I could see it had teeth that looked like sugar cubes. Its eyes was as blood-red as two bullet wounds.

I thought at first it saw us, but after it spit, it turned its head back the way it had been going, and just kept on keeping on; it and that fox and that bear and them weasels. The smell of its spit lingered behind, and it was like the stink of turpentine.

After they was passed, me and Jim got up and started going back through the woods the way we had come, toward the raft. Seeing what we seen had made up our minds for us, and discussion about it wasn't necessary, and I knowed better than to light the lantern again. We just went along and made the best of it in the darkness of the woods.

As we was about to come out of the trees onto the beach, we seen something that froze us in our tracks. Coming along the beach was more of them weasels. Some of them had torches, some of them had clubs, and they all had hats. I guess a weasel don't care for pants, but dearly loves a hat. One of them was carrying a big, wet-looking bag.

We slipped back behind some trees and watched them move along for a bit, but was disappointed to see them stop by the water. They was strung out in a long line, and the weasel with the bag moved in front of the line and the line sort of gathered around him in a horseshoe shape. The weasel put the bag on the ground, opened it, and took out something I couldn't recognize at first. I squatted down so I could see better between their legs, and when I did, I caught my breath. They was passing a man's battered head among them, and they was each sitting down and taking a bite of it, passing it to the next weasel, like they was sharing a big apple.

Jim, who had squatted down beside me, said, "Oh, Huck, chile, look what they doing."

Not knowing what to do, we just stayed there, and then we heard that beating sound we had heard before. Off to our left was a whole batch of torches moving in our direction.

"More of them," Jim said.

Silent, but as quick as we could, we started going away from them. They didn't even know we was there, but they was driving us along like we was wild game 'cause they was looking for that rabbit, I figured.

After a bit, we picked up our pace, because they was closing. As we went more quickly through the woods, two things happened. The woods got thicker and harder to move through, and whatever was behind us started coming faster. I reckoned that was because now they could hear us. It may not have been us they was looking for, but it was darn sure us they was chasing.

It turned into a full-blowed run. I tossed the lantern aside, and we tore through them woods and vines and undergrowth as hard as we could go. Since we wasn't trying to be sneaky about it, Jim was using that cane knife to cut through the hard parts; mostly we just pushed through it.

Then an odd thing happened. We broke out of the woods and was standing on a cliff. Below us, pretty far down, was a big pool of water that the moon's face seemed to be floating on. Across from the pool was more land, and way beyond that was some mountains that rose up so high the peaks looked close to the moon.

I know. It don't make no sense. That island ought not to have been that big. It didn't fit the facts. Course, I reckon in a place where weasels and foxes and bears wear hats, and there's a big ole thing made of a sticky, black mess that spits turpentine, you can expect the facts to have their problems.

Behind us, them weasels was closing, waving torches, and yipping and barking like dogs.

Jim looked at me, said, "We gonna have to jump, Huck. It's all there is for it."

It was a good drop and wasn't no way of knowing what was under that water, but I nodded, aimed for the floating moon and jumped.

It was a quick drop, as it usually is when you step off nothing and fall. Me and Jim hit the water side by side and went under. The water was as cold as a dead man's ass in winter. When we come up swimming and spitting, I lifted my head to look at where we had jumped from. At the edge of the cliff was now the pack of weasels, and they was pressed up together tighter than a cluster of chiggers, leaning over and looking down.

One of them was dedicated, 'cause he jumped with his torch in his hand. He come down right in front of us in the water, went under, and when he come up he still had the torch, but of course it wasn't lit. He swung it and hit Jim upside the head.

Jim had lost the cane knife in the jump, so he didn't have nothing to hit back with. He and the weasel just sort of floated there eyeing one another.

There was a chittering sound from above, as all them weasels rallied their man on. The weasel cocked back the torch again, and swung at me. I couldn't back pedal fast enough, and it caught me a glancing blow on the side of my head. It was a hard enough lick, that for a moment, I not only couldn't swim, I wouldn't have been able to tell you the difference between a cow and a horse and a goat and a cotton sack. Right then, everything seemed pretty much the same to me.

I slipped under, but the water, and me choking on it, brought me back. I clawed my way to the surface, and when I was sort of back to myself, I seen that Jim had the weasel by the neck with one hand, and had its torch arm in his other. The weasel was pretty good sized, but he wasn't as big as Jim, and his neck wasn't on his shoulders as good neither. The weasel had reached its free hand and got Jim's throat and was trying to strangle him; he might as well have been trying to squeeze a tree to death. Jim's fingers dug into the weasel's throat, and there was a sound like someone trying to spit a pea through a tight rolled cigar, and then the next thing I knowed, the weasel was floating like a turd in a night jar.

Above, the pack was still there, and a couple of them threw torches at us, but missed; they hissed out in the water. We swam to the other side, and crawled out.

There was thick brush and woods there, and we staggered into it, with me stopping at the edge of the trees just long enough to yell something nasty to them weasels.

The woods come up along a wall of dirt, and thinned, and there was a small cave in the dirt, and in the cave, sleeping on the floor, was that rabbit we had seen. I doubted it was really a rabbit back then, when we first seen it in the shadows, but after the fox and bear and weasels, and Mr. Sticky, it was hard to doubt anything.

The moonlight was strong enough where the trees had thinned, that we could see the rabbit had white fur and wore a red vest and blue pants and no shoes. He had a pink nose and pink in his big ears, and he was sleeping. He heard us, and in a move so quick it was hard to see, he come awake and sprang to his feet. But we was in front of the cave, blocking the way out.

"Oh, my," he said.

A rabbit speaking right good American was enough to startle both me and Jim. But as I said, this place was the sort of place where you come to expect anything other than a free boat ride home.

Jim said slowly, "Why, I think I know who you are. Uncle Remus talked about you and your red vest. You Brer Rabbit."

The rabbit hung his head and sort of collapsed to the floor of the cave.

"Brer Rabbit," the rabbit said, "that would be me. Well, Fred actually, but when Uncle Remus was here, he knowed me by that name. I had a family once, but they was all eat up. There was Floppsy and Moppsy and Fred, and Alice and Fred Two and Fred Three, and then there was, oh, I don't even remember now, it's been so long ago they was eaten up, or given to Cut Through You."

There was a roll of thunder, and rain started darting down on us. We went inside the cave with Brer Rabbit and watched lightning cut across the sky and slam into what looked like a sycamore tree.

"Lightning," Jim said, to no one in particular. "It don't leave no shadow. You got a torch, it leaves a shadow. The sun makes a shadow on the ground of things it shines on. But lightning, it don't leave no shadow."

"No," Brer Rabbit said, looking up and out of the cave. "It don't, and it never has. And here, on this island, when it starts to rain and the lightning flashes and hits the ground like that, it's a warning. It means time is closing out. But what makes it bad is there's something new now. Something really awful."

"The weasels, you mean," Jim said.

"No," Brer Rabbit said. "Something much worse."

"Well," Jim said, "them weasels is bad enough. We seen them eating a man's head."

"Riverboat captain probably," Brer Rabbit said. "Big ole steamboat got too close and got sucked in. And then there was the lady in the big, silver mosquito."

"Beg your pardon," I said.

"Well, it reminded me of a mosquito. I ain't got no other way to explain it, so I won't. But that head, it was probably all that remains of that captain. It could have been some of the others, but I reckon it was him. He had a fat head."

"How do you know all this?" I said.

Brer Rabbit looked at me, pulled his paw from behind his back, where he had been keeping it, and we saw he didn't have a hand on the end of it. Course, he didn't have a hand on the one showing neither. He had a kind of paw with fingers, which is the best I can describe it, but that other arm ended in a nubbin.

The rabbit dropped his head then, let his arm fall to his side, like everything inside of him had turned to water and run out on the ground. "I know what happened 'cause I was there, and was gonna be one of the sacrifices. Would have been part of the whole thing had I not gnawed my paw off. It was the only way out. While I was doing it, it hurt like hell, but I kept thinking, rabbit meat, it ain't so bad. Ain't that a thing to think? It still hurts. I been running all night. But it ain't no use. I am a shadow of my former self. Was a time when I was clever and smart, but these days I ain't neither one. They gonna catch up with me now. I been outsmarting them for years, but everything done got its time, and I reckon mine has finally come. Brer Fox, he's working up to the Big One, and tonight could be the night it all comes down in a bad way. If ole Cut Through You gets enough souls."

"I'm so confused I feel turned around and pulled inside out," I said.

"I'm a might confused myself," Jim said.

The rain was really hammering now. The lightning was tearing at the sky and poking down hot yellow forks, hitting trees, catching them on fire. It got so there were so many burning, that the inside of our cave was lit up for a time like it was daylight.

"This here rain," Brer Rabbit said. "They don't like it. Ain't nobody likes it, 'cause that lightning can come down on your ass sure as it can on a tree. The Warning Rain we call it. Means that there ain't much time before the next rain comes. The Soft Rain, and when it does, it's that time. Time to go."

"I just thought I was confused before," I said.

"All right," Brer Rabbit said. "It ain't like we're going anywhere now, and it ain't like they'll be coming. They'll be sheltering up somewhere nearby to get out of the Warning Rain. So, I'll tell you what you want to know. Just ask."

"I'll make it easy," I said. "Tell us all of it."

And he did. Now, no disrespect to Brer Rabbit, but once he got going, he was a dad burn blabbermouth. He told us all we wanted to know, and all manner of business we didn't want to know. I think it's best I just summarize what he was saying, keeping in mind it's possible I've left out some of the important parts, but mostly, I can assure you, I've left out stuff you don't want to hear anyway. We even got a few pointers on how to decorate a burrow, which seemed to be a tip we didn't need.

The rain got so thick it put those burning trees out, and with the moon behind clouds, it was dark in that cave. We couldn't even see each other. All we could do was hear Brer Rabbit's voice, which was a little squeaky.

What he was telling us was, there was gonna be some kind of ceremony. That whoever the weasels could catch was gonna be a part of it. It wasn't no ceremony where there was cake and prizes and games, least not any that was fun. It was gonna be a ceremony in honor of this fella he called Cut Through You.

According to Brer Rabbit, the island wasn't always a bad place. He and his family had lived here, along with all the other brother and sister animals, or whatever the hell they were, until Brer Fox found the stones and the book wrapped in skin. That's how Brer Rabbit put it. The book wrapped in skin.

Brer Fox, he wasn't never loveable, and Brer Rabbit said right up front, he used to pull tricks on him and Brer Bear all the time. They was harmless, he said, and they was mostly just to keep from getting eaten by them two. 'Cause as nice a place as it was then as measured up against now, it was still a place where meat eaters lived alongside them that wasn't meat eaters, which meant them that ate vegetables was the meat eater's lunch, if they got caught. Brer Rabbit said he figured that was just fair play. That was how the world worked, even if their island wasn't exactly like the rest of the world.

It dropped out of the sky come the full moon and ended up in the big wide middle of the Mississippi. It stayed that way for a few hours, and then come the Warning Rain, as he called it, the one we was having now; the one full of lighting and thunder and hard falling water. It meant they was more than halfway through their time to be on the Mississippi, then there was gonna come the Soft Rain. It didn't have no lighting in it. It was pleasant. At least until the sky opened up and the wind came down and carried them away.

"Where does it take you?" I asked.

Brer Rabbit shook his head. "I don't know I can say. We don't seem to know nothing till we come back. And when we do, well, we just pick up right where we was before. Doing whatever it was we was doing. So if Brer Fox has me by the neck, and the time comes, and we all get sucked away, when it blows back, we gonna be right where we was; it's always night and always like things was when we left them."

He said when that funnel of wind dropped them back on the island, sometimes it brought things with it that wasn't there before. Like people from other places. Other worlds, he said. That didn't make no sense at all to me. But that's what he said. He said sometimes it brought live people, and sometimes it brought dead people, and sometimes it brought Brer People with it, and sometimes what it brought wasn't people at all. He told us about some big old crawdads come through once, and how they chased everyone around, but ended up being boiled in water and eaten by Brer Bear, Brer Fox, and all the weasels, who was kind of butt kissers to Brer Fox.

Anyway, not knowing what was gonna show up on the island, either by way of that Sticky Storm—as he named it 'cause everything clung to it—or by way of the Mississippi, made things interesting; right before it got too interesting. The part that was too interesting had to do with Brer Fox and that Book of Skin.

Way Brer Rabbit figured, it come through that hole in the sky like everything else. It was clutched in a man's hand, and the man was deader than a rock, and he had what Brer Rabbit said was a towel or a rag or some such thing wrapped around his head.

Brer Rabbit said he seen that dead man from a hiding place in the woods, and Uncle Remus was with him when he did. Uncle Remus had escaped slavery and come to the island. He fit in good. Stayed in the burrow with Brer Rabbit and his family, and he listened to all their stories.

But when the change come, when that book showed up, and stuff started happening because of it, he decided he'd had enough and tried to swim back to shore. Things he saw made him think taking his chance on drowning, or getting caught and being a slave again, was worth it. I don't know how he felt later, but he sure got caught, since Jim knew him and had heard stories about Dread Island from him.

"He left before things really got bad," Brer Rabbit said. "And did they get bad. He was lucky."

"That depends on how you look at it," Jim said. "I done been a slave, and I can't say it compares good to much of anything."

"Maybe," Brer Rabbit said. "Maybe."

And then he went on with his story.

Seems that when the storm brought that dead man clutching that book, Brer Fox pried it out of his hands and opened it up and found it was written in some foreign language, but he could read it. Brer Rabbit said one of the peculiars about the island is that everyone—except the weasels, who pretty much got the short end of the stick when it come to smarts—could read or speak any language there was.

Now, wasn't just the book and the dead man come through, there was the stones. They had fallen out of the sky at the same time. There was also a mass of black goo with dying and dead fish in it that come through, and it splattered all over the ground. The stones was carved up. The main marking was a big eye, then there was all manner of other scratchings and drawings. And though the Brer Folk could read or speak any language possible, even the language in that book, they couldn't speak or read what was on them stones. It had been put together by folk spoke a tongue none of their mouths would fit around. Least at first.

Brer Fox went to holding that book dear. Everyone on the island knew about it, and he always carried it in a pack on his back. Brer Bear, who was kind of a kiss ass like the weasels, but smarter than they was—and, according to Brer Rabbit, that was a sad thing to think about, since Brer Bear didn't hardly have the sense to get in out of the Warning Rain—helped Brer Fox set them stones up in that black muck. Every time the storm brought them back, that's what they did, and pretty soon they had the weasels helping them.

Fact was, Brer Fox all but quit chasing Brer Rabbit. He instead sat and read by firelight and moonlight, and started chanting, 'cause he was learning how to say that language that he couldn't read before, the language on the stones, and he was teaching Brer Bear how to do the same. And one time, well, the island stayed overnight.

"It didn't happen but that once," Brer Rabbit said. "But come daylight, here we still was. And it stayed that way until the next night come, and finally before next morning, things got back to the way they was supposed to be. Brer Fox had some power from that book and those stones, and he liked it mighty good."

Now and again he'd chant something from the book, and the air would fill with an odor like rotting fish, and then that odor got heavy and went to whirling about them stones; it was an odor that made the stomach crawl and the head fill with all manner of sickness and worry and grief.

Once, while Brer Rabbit was watching Brer Fox chant, while he was smelling that rotten fish stink, he saw the sky crack open, right up close by the moon. Not the way it did when the Sticky Storm come, which was when everything turned gray and the sky opened up and a twister of sorts dropped down and sucked them all up. It was more like the night sky was just a big black sheet, and this thing with one, large, nasty, rolling eye and more legs than a spider—and ropey legs at that— poked through and pulled at the night.

For a moment, Brer Rabbit thought that thing—which from Brer Fox's chanting he learned was called Cut Through You—was gonna take hold of the moon and eat it like a flap jack. It had a odd mouth with a beak, and it was snapping all the while.

Then, sudden like, it was sucked back, like something got hold of one of its legs and yanked it plumb out of sight. The sky closed up and the air got clean for a moment, and it was over with.

After that, Brer Fox and ole One Eye had them a connection. Every time the island was brought back, Brer Fox would go out there and stand in that muck, or sit on a rock in the middle of them carved stones, and call out to Cut Through You. It was a noise, Brer Rabbit said, sounded like someone straining at toilet while trying to cough and yodel all at the same time.

Brer Fox and Brer Bear was catching folk and tying them to the stones. People from the Mississippi come along by accident; they got nabbed too, mostly by the weasels. It was all so Brer Fox could have Cut Through You meetings.

Way it was described to me, it was kind of like church. Except when it come time to pass the offering, the sky would crack open, and ole Cut Through You would lean out and reach down and pull folk tied to the stones up there with him.

Brer Rabbit said he watched it eat a bunch a folk quicker than a mule skinner could pop goober peas; chawed them up and spat them out, splattered what was left in that black mud that was all around the stones.

That was what Brer Fox and Brer Bear, and all them weasels, took to eating. It changed them. They went from sneaky and hungry and animal like, to being more like men. Meaning, said Brer Rabbit, they come to enjoy cruelty. And then Brer Fox built the Tar Baby, used that book to give it life. It could do more work than all of them put together, and it set up the final stones by itself. Something dirty needed to be done, it was Tar Baby done it. You couldn't stop the thing, Brer Rabbit said. It just kept on a coming, and a coming.

But the final thing Brer Rabbit said worried him, was that each time Cut Through You came back, there's more and more of him to be seen, and it turned out there's a lot more of Cut Through You than you'd think; and it was like he was hungrier each time he showed.

Bottom line, as figured by Brer Rabbit, was this: if Brer Fox and his bunch didn't supply the sacrifices, pretty soon they'd be sacrifices themselves.

Brer Rabbit finished up his story, and it was about that time the rain quit. The clouds melted away and the moonlight was back. It was clear out, and you could see a right smart distance.

I said, "You ain't seen a couple of fellas named Tom and Joe, have you? One of them might be wearing a straw hat. They're about my age and size, but not quite as good looking."

Brer Rabbit shook his head. "I ain't," he said. "But they could be with all the others Brer Fox has nabbed of late. Was they on the riverboat run aground?"

I shook my head.

Jim said, "Huck, you and me, we got to get back to the raft and get on out of this place, Tom and Joe or not."

"That's right," Brer Rabbit said. "You got to. Oh, I wish I could go with you."

"You're invited," I said.

"Ah, but there is the thorn in the paw. I can't go, 'cause I do, come daylight, if I ain't on this island, I disappear, and I don't come back. Though to tell you true, that might be better than getting ate up by Cut Through You. I'll give it some considering."

"Consider quick," Jim said, "we got to start back to the raft."

"What we got to do," Brer Rabbit said, "is we got to go that way."

He pointed.

"Then," he said, "we work down to the shore, and you can get your raft. And I'm thinking I might just go with you and turn to nothing. I ain't got no family now. I ain't got nothing but me, and part of me is missing, so the rest of me might as well go missing too."

Jim said, "I got my medicine bag with me. I can't give you your paw back, but I can take some of the hurt away with a salve I got."

Jim dressed Brer Rabbit's paw, and when that was done, he got some wool string out of that little bag he had on his belt and tied up his hair—which had grown long—in little sheaves, like dark wheat. He said it was a thing to do to keep back witches.

I pointed out witches seemed to me the least of our worries, but he done it anyway, with me taking my pocketknife out of my back pocket to cut the string for him.

When he had knotted his hair up in about twenty gatherings, we lit out for the raft without fear of witches.

Way we went made it so we had to swim across a creek that was deep in places. It was cold water, like that blue hole we had jumped in, and there was fish in it. They was curious and would bob to the top and look at us; their eyes was shiny as wet stones in the moonlight.

On the other side of the creek, we stumbled through a patch of woods, and down a hill, and then up one that led us level with where we had been before. In front of us was more dark woods. Brer Rabbit said beyond the trees was the shore-line, and we might be able to get to our raft if the weasels hadn't found it. Me and

Jim decided if they had, we'd try for Tom's and Joe's boat and wish them our best. If their boat was gone, then, there was nothing left but to hit that Mississippi and swim for it. We had about as much chance of making that swim as passing through the eye of a needle, but it was a might more inviting than Cut Through You. Least, that way we had a chance. Me and Jim was both good swimmers, and maybe we could even find a log to push off into the water with us. As for Brer Rabbit, well, he was thinking on going with us and just disappearing when daylight come; that was a thing made me really want to get off that island. If he was willing to go out that way, then that Cut Through You must be some nasty sort of fella. Worse yet, our salt had got all wet and wasn't worth nothing, and we had both lost the cross in our shoes. All we had was those rusty nails on strings, and I didn't have a whole lot of trust in that. I was more comfortable that I still had my little knife in my back pocket.

We was coming down through the woods, and it got so the trees were thinning, and we could see the bank down there, the river churning along furious like. My heart was starting to beat in an excited way, and about then, things turned to dog doo.

The weasels come down out of the trees on ropes, and a big net come down with them and landed over us. It was weighed down with rocks, and there wasn't no time to get out from under it before they was tugging it firm around us, and we was bagged up tighter than a strand of gut packed with sausage makings.

As we was laying there, out of the woods come Brer Fox and Brer Bear. They come right over to us. The fox bent down, and he looked Brer Rabbit in the eye. He grinned and showed his teeth. His breath was so sour we could smell it from four feet away; it smelled like death warmed over and gone cold again.

Up close, I could see things I couldn't see before in the night. He had fish scales running along the side of his face, and when he breathed there were flaps that flared out on his cheeks; they was gills, like a fish.

I looked up at Brer Bear. There were sores all over his body, and bits of fish heads and fish tails poking out of him like moles. He was breathing in and out, like bellows being worked to start up a fresh fire.

"You ain't looking so good," Brer Rabbit said.

"Yeah," Brer Fox said, "but looks ain't everything. I ain't looking so good, but you ain't doing so good."

Brer Fox slung his pack off his back and opened it. I could see there was a book in there, the one bound up in human skin. You could see there was a face on the cover, eyes, nose, mouth, and some warts. But that wasn't what Brer Fox was reaching for. What he was reaching for was Brer Rabbit's paw, which was stuffed in there.

"Here's a little something you left back at the ceremony spot." He held up the paw and waved it around. "That wasn't nice. I had plans for you. But, you know what? I got a lucky rabbit's foot now. Though, to tell the truth, it ain't all that lucky for you, is it?"

He put the paw in his mouth and clamped down on it and bit right through it and chewed on it some. He gave what was left of it to Brer Bear, who ate it up in one big bite.

"I figured you wouldn't be needing it," Brer Fox said.

"Why, I'm quite happy with this nubbing," Brer Rabbit said. "I don't spend so much time cleaning my nails now."

Brer Fox's face turned sour, like he had bitten into an unripe persimmon. "There ain't gonna be nothing of you to clean after tonight. And in fact, we got to go quick like. I wouldn't want you to miss the meeting, Brer Rabbit. You see, tonight, he comes all the way through, and then, me and my folk, we're gonna serve him. He's gonna go all over the Mississippi, and then all over the world. He's gonna rule, and I'm gonna rule beside him. He told me. He told me in my head."

With those last words, Brer Fox tapped the side of his head with a finger.

"You gonna get ate up like everyone else," Brer Rabbit said. "You just a big ole idiot."

Brer Fox rose up, waved his hand over his head, yelled out, "Bring them. And don't be easy about it. Let's blood them."

What that meant was they dragged us in that net. We was pressed up tight together, and there was all manner of stuff on the ground to stick us, and we banged into trees and such, and it seemed like forever before we broke out of the woods and I got a glimpse at the place we was going.

Right then I knew why it was Brer Rabbit would rather just disappear.

We was scratched and bumped up and full of ticks and chiggers and poison ivy by the time we got to where we was going, and where we was going didn't have no trees and there wasn't nothing pretty about it.

There was this big stretch of black mud. You could see dead fish in it, and some of them was mostly bones, but there were still some flopping about. They were fish I didn't recognize. Some had a lot of eyes and big teeth and were shaped funny.

Standing up in the mud were these big dark slabs of rock that wasn't quite black and wasn't quite brown, but was somewhere between any color you can mention. The moonlight laid on them like a slick of bacon grease, and you could see markings all over them. Each and every one of them had a big ole eye at the top of the slab, and below it were all manner of marks. Some of the marks looked like fish or things with lots of legs, and beaks, and then there was marks that didn't look like nothing but chicken scratch. But, I can tell you this, looking at those slabs and those marks made my stomach feel kind of funny, like I had swallowed a big chaw of tobacco right after eating too many hot peppers and boiled pig's feet, something, by the way, that really happened to me once.

Standing out there in that black muck was the weasels. On posts all around the muck right where it was still solid ground, there was men and women with their hands tied behind their backs and then tied to rings on the posts. I reckoned a number of them was from the steamboat wreck. There was also a woman wearing a kind of leather cap, and she had on pants just like a man. She was kind of pretty, and where everyone else was hanging their heads, she looked mad as a hornet. As we was pulled up closer to the muck, I saw that Tom and Joe was there, tied to posts, drooping like flowers too long in the hot sun, missing Bowie knife, gun, and packed lunch.

When they seen me and Jim, they brightened for a second, then realized wasn't nothing we could do, and that we was in the same situation as them. It hurt me to see Tom like that, all sagging. It was the first time I'd ever seen seen him about given up. Like us, they was all scratched up and even in the moonlight, you could see they was spotted like speckled pups from bruises.

Out behind them I could see parts of that big briar patch we had seen when we first sailed our raft onto the island. The briars twisted up high, and the way the moonlight fell into them, that whole section looked like a field of coiled ropes and nails. I hadn't never seen a briar patch like that before.

There were some other things out there in the muck that I can't explain, and there was stuff on the sides of where the muck ended. I figured, from what Brer Rabbit had told us, they was stuff from them other worlds or places that sometimes come through on the Sticky Storm. One of them things was a long boat of sorts, but it had wings on it, and it was shiny silver and had a tail on it like a fish. There was some kind of big crosses on the wings, and it was just sitting on wheels over on some high grass, but the wheels wasn't like any I'd ever seen on a wagon or buggy.

There was also this big thing looked like a gourd, if a gourd could be about a thousand times bigger; it was stuck up in the mud with the fat part down, and the thinner part in the air, and it had little fins on it. Written on it in big writing was something that didn't make no sense to me. It said: HOWDY ALL YOU JAPS.

Wasn't a moment or two passed between me seeing all this, then we was being pulled out of the net and carried over to three empty posts. A moment later, they wasn't empty no more. We was tied to the wooden rings on them tight as a fishing knot.

I turned my head and looked at Jim.

He said, "You're right, they ain't no witch problems around here."

"Maybe," I said, "it's because of the string. Who knows how many witches would be around otherwise."

Jim grinned at me. "That's right. That's right, ain't it?"

I nodded and smiled at him. I figured if we was gonna be killed, and wasn't nothing we could do about it, we might as well try and be cheerful.

Right then, coming across that black mud, its feet splattering and sucking in the muck as it pulled them free for each step, was the Tar Baby.

Now that he was out under the moonlight, I could see he was stuck all over with what at first looked like long needles, but as he come closer, I saw was straw. He was shot through with it. I figured it was a thing Brer Fox used to help put him together, mixing it with tar he got from somewhere, and turpentine, and maybe some things I didn't want to know about; you could smell that turpentine as he waddled closer, spitting all the while.

He sauntered around the circle of folks that was tied to the posts, and as he did, his plump belly would flare open, and you could see fire in there and bits of ash and bones being burned up along with fish heads and a human skull. Tar Baby went by each of them on the posts and pushed his face close to their faces so he could enjoy how they curled back from him. I knew a bully when I seen one, 'cause I had fought a few, and when I was younger, I was kind of a bully my-self, till a girl named Hortense Miller beat the snot out of me, twisted my arm behind my back and made me say cotton sack, and even then, after I said it, she made me eat a mouthful of dirt and tell her I liked it. She wasn't one to settle an argument easy like. It cured my bully days.

When the Tar Baby come to me and pushed his face close, I didn't flinch. I just looked him in his red eyes like they was nothing, even though it was all I could do to keep my knees from chattering together. He stayed looking at me for a long time, then grunted, left the air around me full of the fog and stink of turpentine. Jim was next, and Jim didn't flinch none either. That didn't set well with Tar Baby, two rascals in a row, so he reached out with a finger and poked Jim's chest. There was a hissing sound and smoke come off Jim. That made me figure he was being burned by the Tar Baby somehow, but when the Tar Baby pulled his chubby tar finger back, it was him that was smoking.

I leaned out and took a good look and seen the 'cause of it—the nail on the string around Jim's neck. The Tar Baby had poked it and that iron nail had actually worked its magic on him. Course, problem was, he had to put his finger right on it, but in that moment, I gathered me a more favorable view of the hoodoo methods.

Tar Baby looked at the end of his smoking finger, like he might find something special there, then he looked at Jim, and his mouth twisted. I think he was gonna do something nasty, but there come a rain all of a sudden. The Soft Rain Brer Rabbit told us about. It come down sweet smelling and light and warm. No thunder. No lightning. And no clouds. Just water falling out of a clear sky stuffed with stars and a big fat moon; it was the rain that was supposed to let everyone know it wouldn't be long before daylight and the Sticky Storm.

The weasels and Brer Fox and Brer Bear, and that nasty Tar Baby, all made their way quick like to the tallest stone in the muck. They stood in front of it, and you could tell they was nervous, even the Tar Baby, and they went about chanting. The words were like someone spitting and sucking and coughing and clearing their throat all at once, if they was words at all. This went on for a while, and wasn't nothing happening but that rain, which was kind of pleasant.

"Huck," Jim said, "you done been as good a friend as man could have, and I ain't happy you gonna die, or me neither, but we got to, it makes me happy knowing you gonna go out with me."

"I'd feel better if you was by yourself," I said, and Jim let out a cackle when I said it.

There was a change in things, a feeling that the air had gone heavy. I looked up and the rain fell on my face and ran in my mouth and tasted good. The night sky was vibrating a little, like someone shaking weak pudding in a bowl. Then the sky cracked open like Brer Rabbit had told us about, and I seen there was light up there in the crack. It was light like you'd see from a lantern behind a wax paper curtain. After a moment, something moved behind the light, and then something moved in front of it. A dark shape about the size of the moon; the moon itself was starting to drift low and thin off to the right of the island.

Brer Rabbit had tried to describe it to us, ole Cut Through You, but all I can say is there ain't no real way to tell you how it looked, 'cause there wasn't nothing to measure it against. It was big and it had one eye that was dark and unblinking, and it had a beak of sorts, and there were all these ropey arms; but the way it looked shifted and changed so much you couldn't get a real handle on it.

I won't lie to you. It wasn't like standing up to the Tar Baby. My knees started knocking together, and my heart was beating like a drum and my insides felt as if they were being worked about like they was in a milk churn. Them snaky arms on that thing was clawing at the sky, and I even seen the sky give on the sides, like it was about to rip all over and fall down.

I pressed my back against the post, and when I did, I felt that pocketknife in my back pocket. It come to me then that if I stuck out my butt a little and pulled the rope loose as possible on the ring I was tied to, I might be able to thumb that knife out of my pocket, so I give it a try.

It wasn't easy, but that thing up there gave me a lot of will power. I worked the knife with my thumb and long finger, and got it out, and flicked it open, and turned it in my hand, almost dropping it. When that happened, it felt like my heart had leaped down a long tunnel somewhere. But when I knew I still had it, I turned it and went to cutting. Way I was holding it, twisted so that it come back against the rope on the ring, I was doing a bit of work on my wrists as well as the tie. It was a worrying job, but I stayed at it, feeling blood running down my hands.

While I was at it, that chanting got louder and louder, and I seen off to the side of Cut Through You, another hole opening up in the sky; inside that hole it looked like a whirlpool, like you find in the river; it was bright as day in that hole, and the day was churning around and around and the sky was widening.

I figured then the ceremony was in a kind of hurry, 'cause Cut Through You was peeking through, and that whirling hole was in competition to him. He wouldn't have nothing to eat and no chanting to hear, if the Sticky Storm took everyone away first.

You see, it was the chanting that was helping Cut Through You get loose. It gave him strength, hearing that crazy language.

From where we was, I could see the pink of the morning starting to lay across the far end of the river, pushing itself up like the bloom of a rose, and that ole moon dipping down low, like a wheel of rat cheese being slowly lowered into a sack.

So, there we were, Cut Through You thrashing around in the sky, the Sticky Storm whirling about, and the sun coming up. The only thing that would have made it worse was if I had had to pee.

Everything started to shake, and I guess that was because Cut Through You and that storm was banging together in some way behind night's curtain, and maybe the sun starting to rise had something to do with it. The Sticky Storm dipped out of that hole and it come down lower. I could see all manner of stuff up there in it, but I couldn't make out none of it. It looked like someone had taken some different mixes of paint and thrown them all together; a few light things on the ground started to float up toward the storm, and when they did, I really understood why Brer Rabbit called it a Sticky Storm; it was like it was fly paper and all that was sucked up got stuck to it like flies.

About then, I cut that rope in two, and pulled my bleeding hands loose. I ran over to Jim and cut him loose.

Brer Fox and the others didn't even notice. They was so busy looking up at Cut Through You. I didn't have the time, but I couldn't help but look up too. It had its head poking all the way through, and that head was so big you can't imagine, and it was lumpy and such, like a bunch of melons had been put in a tow sack and banged on with a boat paddle; it was leaking green goo that was falling down on the ground, and onto the worshipers, and they was grabbing it off the muck, or off themselves, and sticking their fingers in their mouths and licking them clean.

It didn't look like what the Widow Douglas would have called sanitary, and I could see that them that was eating it, was starting to change. Sores, big and bloody, was popping up on them like a rash.

I ran on around the circle to Tom and Joe and cut them loose, and then we all run back the other way, 'cause as much as I'd like to have helped them on that farther part of the circle, it was too late. On that side the ground was starting to fold up, and their posts was coming loose. It was like someone had taken a sheet of paper and curled one end of it. They was being sucked up in the sky toward that Sticky Storm, and even the black mud was coming loose and shooting up in the sky.

On the other end of the circle, things was still reasonably calm, so I rushed to Brer Rabbit and cut him loose, then that lady with the pants on. Right about then, Cut Through You let out with a bellow so loud it made the freckles on my butt crawl up my back and hide in my hair, or so it felt. Wasn't no need to guess that Cut Through You was mad that he was running out of time, and he was ready to take it out on most anybody. He stuck long ropey legs out of the sky and went to thrashing at Brer Fox and the others. I had the pleasure of seeing Brer Fox getting his head snapped off, and then Brer Bear was next.

The weasels, not being of strong stuff to begin with, starting running like rats from a sinking ship. But it didn't do them no good. That Cut Through You's legs was all over them, grabbing their heads and jerking them off, and them that wasn't beheaded, was being pulled up in the sky by the Sticky Storm.

I was still on that side of the circle, cutting people loose, and soon as I did, a bunch of them just ran wildly, some right into the storm. They was yanked up, and went out of sight. All of the island seemed like it was wadding up.

Brer Rabbit grabbed my shoulder, said, "It's every man for his self," and then he darted along the edge of the Sticky Storm, dashed between two whipping Cut Through You legs, and leaped right into that briar patch, which seemed crazy to me. All the while he's running and jumping in the briars, I'm yelling, "Brer Rabbit, come back."

But he didn't. I heard him say, "Born and raised in the briar patch, born and raised," and then he was in the big middle of it, even as it was starting to fold up and get pulled toward the sky.

Now that we was free, I didn't know what to do. There didn't seem no place to go. Even the shoreline was starting to curl up.

Jim was standing by me. He said, "I reckon this is it, Huck. I say we let that storm take us, and not Cut Through You."

We was about to go right into the storm, 'cause the side of it wasn't but a few steps away, when I got my elbow yanked. I turned and it was Tom Sawyer, and Joe with him.

"The lady," Tom said. "This way."

I turned and seen the shorthaired lady was at that silver boat, and she was waving us to her. Any port in a storm, so to speak, so we run toward her with Tom and Joe. A big shadow fell over us as we run, and then a leg come popping out of the sky like a whip, and caught Joe around the neck, and yanked his head plumb off. His headless body must have run three or four steps before it went down.

I heard Tom yell out, and stop, as if to help the body up. "You got to run for it, Tom," I said. "Ain't no other way. Joe's deader than last Christmas."

So we come up on the silver boat with the wings, and there was an open door in the side of it, and we rushed in there and closed it. The lady was up front in a seat, behind this kind of partial wheel, looking out through a glass that run in front of her. The silver bug was humming, and those crosses on the wings was spinning. She touched something and let loose of something else, and we started to bounce, and then we was running along on the grass. I moved to the seat beside her, and she glanced over at me. She was white faced, but determined looking.

"That was Noonan's seat," she said.

I didn't know what to say to that. I didn't know if I should get out of it or not, but I'll tell you, I didn't. I couldn't move. And then we was bouncing harder, and the island was closing in on us, and Cut Through You's rope legs was waving around us. One of them got hit by the crosses, which was spinning so fast you could hardly make them out. They hit it, and the winged boat was knocked a bit. The leg come off in a spray of green that splattered on the glass, and then the boat started to lift up. I can't explain it, and I know it ain't believable, but we was flying.

The sun was really starting to brighten things now, and as we climbed up, I seen the woods was still in front of us. The lady was trying to make the boat go higher, but I figured we was gonna clip the top of them trees and end up punched to death by them, but then the boat rose up some, and I could feel and hear the trees brush against the bottom of it, like someone with a whisk broom snapping dust off a coat collar.

With the island curing up all around us and starting to come apart in a spray of color, being sucked up by the Sticky Storm, and that flying boat wobbling and a rattling, I figured we had done all this for nothing.

The boat turned slightly, like the lady was tacking a sail. I could glance up and out of the glass and see Cut Through You. He was sticking his head out of a pink morning sky, and his legs was thrashing, but he didn't look so big now; it was like the light had shrunk him up. I seen Tar Baby too, or what was left of him, and he was splattering against that big gourd thing with the writing on it, splattering like someone was flicking ink out of a writing pen. He and that big gourd was whipping around us like angry bugs.

Then there was a feeling like we was an arrow shot from a bow, and the boat jumped forward, and then it went up high, turned slightly, and below I seen the island was turning into a ball, and the ball was starting to look wet. Then it, the rain, every dang thing, including ole Cut Through You, who was sucked out of his hole, shot up into that Sticky Storm.

Way we was now, I could still see Tar Baby splashed on that gourd, and the gourd started to shake, then it twisted and went as flat as a tape worm, and for some reason, it blowed; it was way worse than dynamite. When it blew up, it threw some Tar Baby on the flying boat's glass. The boat started to shake and the air inside and out had blue ripples in it.

And then—

—the island was gone and there was just the Mississippi below us. Things was looking good for a minute, and then the boat started coughing, and black smoke come up from that whirly thing that had cut off one of Cut Through You's legs.

The boat dropped, the lady pulling at that wheel, yanking at doo-dads and such, but having about as much luck taking us back up as I'd have had trying to lift a dead cow off the ground by the tail.

"We are going down," she said, as if this might not be something we hadn't noticed. "And there is nothing else to do but hope for the best."

Well, to make a long story short. She was right.

Course, hope only goes so far.

She fought that boat all the way down, and then it hit the water and skipped like it was a flat rock. We skipped and skipped, then the whirly gigs flew off, and one of them smashed the glass. I was thrown out of the seat, and around the inside of the boat like a ball.

Then everything knotted up, and there was a bang on my head, and the next thing I know there's water all over. The boat was about half full inside. I suppose that's what brought me around, that cold Mississippi water.

The glass up front was broke open, and water was squirting in around the edges, so I helped it by giving it a kick. It come loose at the edges, and I was able to push it out with my feet. Behind me was Tom Sawyer, and he come from the back like a farm mule in sight of the barn. Fact was, he damn near run over me going through the hole I'd made.

By the time he got through, there wasn't nothing but water, and I was holding my breath. Jim grabbed me from below, and pushed me by the seat of my pants through the hole. Then it was like the boat was towed out from under me. Next thing I knew I was on top of the water floating by Tom, spitting and coughing.

"Jim," I said, "where's Jim?"

"Didn't see him come up," Tom said.

"I guess not," I said. "You was too busy stepping on my head on your way out of that flying boat."

Tom started swimming toward shore, and I just stayed where I was, dog paddling, looking for Jim. I didn't see him, but on that sunlit water there come a big bubble and a burst of something black as the tar baby had been. It spread over the water. It was oil. I could smell it.

Next thing, I felt a tug at my leg. I thought it was one of them big catfish grabbing me, but it wasn't. It was Jim. He bobbed up beside me, and I grabbed him and hugged him and he hugged me back.

"I tried to save her, Huck. I did. But she was done dead. I could tell when I touched her, she was done dead."

"You done what you could."

"What about Tom?" Jim said.

I nodded in the direction Tom had gone swimming. We could see his arms going up and down in the water, swimming like he thought he could make the far shore in about two minutes.

Wasn't nothing to do, but for us to start swimming after him. We done that for a long time, floating some, swimming some. And I'm ashamed to say Jim had to pull me along a few times, 'cause I got tuckered out.

When we was both about gone under, a big tree come floating by, and we climbed up on it. We seen Tom wasn't too far away, having gotten slower as he got tired. We yelled for him, and he come swimming back. The water flow was slow right then, and he caught up with us pretty quick, which is a good thing, 'cause if he hadn't, he'd have sure enough drowned. We clung and floated, and it was late that afternoon when we finally was seen by some fishermen and pulled off the log and into their boat.

There isn't much left to tell. All I can say is we was tired for three days, and when we tried to tell our story, folks just laughed at us. Didn't believe us at all. Course, can't blame them, as I'm prone toward being a liar.

It finally got so we had to tell a lie for it to be believed for the truth, and that included Tom who was in on it with us. We had to say Joe drowned, because they wouldn't believe Cut Through You jerked his head off. They didn't believe there was a Cut Through You. Even the folks believed there was a Dread Island didn't believe our story.

Tom and Becky got together, and they been together ever since. Five years have passed, and dang if Tom didn't become respectable and marry Becky. They got a kid now. But maybe they ain't all that respectable. I count eight months from the time they married until the time their bundle of joy come along.

Last thing I reckon I ought to say, is every year I go out to the edge of the Mississippi with Jim and toss some flowers on the water in memory of the lady who flew us off the island in that winged boat.

As for Dread Island. Well, here's something odd. I can't see it no more, not even when it's supposed to be there.

Jim says it might be my eyes, 'cause when you get older you lose sight of some things you used to could see.

I don't know. But I think it ain't out there no time anymore, and it might not be coming back. I figure it, Brer Rabbit and Cut Through You is somewhere else that ain't like nothing else we know. If that's true, all I got to say, is I hope Brer Rabbit is hid up good, far away from Cut Through You, out there in the thorns, out there where he was raised, in the deep parts of that big old briar patch.

Quoth the Rock Star

By

Rio Youers

The Lyric Theater, Baltimore, MD.
Friday October 13, 1967.

They described him as electrifying and passionate—a rock shaman charged with a dark, sexual energy that left the audience breathless. They used adjectives and superlatives that, while approbative, meant nothing to Jim. He slithered across the stage, trapped in the lights like a lizard in the sun, and vocalized from the depths of his soul. He looked at their faces and heard them calling—*screaming*—his name. They held out their hands, as pale as flowers. They threw their energy at him, and he held it, and cast it back in crashing black waves.

Electrifying.

Passionate.

Rock shaman.

He wrote lyrics—splashed his soul to music—to entertain their intellect, and to offer glimpses of his mind. He was a poet, through and through. The performances were recitations; dark verse married to melody. A war raged in Vietnam and every other band clapped their hands and placed flowers in their hair. His band rode the snake. They sermonized from a barely imagined rim where the day destroyed the night. They sang about fire and death ... The End. They were a four-man orchestra, bleeding dark colors. They created symphonies of psychedelia and challenged their audience to break on through. But for the most part, all they saw—this audience, with their pale-flower hands and flashing cameras—all they saw was a drummer, a guitarist, a keyboardist, and a charismatic, enigmatic lead singer with a pretty face.

They saw nothing.

Jim Morrison sprawled on the stage of the Lyric Theater, motionless, held in the moment like something painted. A fallen leaf, perhaps, curled and brown. Or a still river: deep, uncertain waters. The crowd chanted his name and he looked at them from his prone position, but saw little through the stage lights' glare. He had dropped acid before the show and he could feel it biting the corners of his consciousness. There was a black, velvet curtain in front of him and beyond it the audience roared. Not individuals, but a singular entity: a massive mouth gushing nonsense, filled with teeth. The stage vibrated with the band's extemporization. He could feel it through his cheekbone and ribcage, and in the delicate plates of his skull. He closed his eyes and felt the music. Ray's fingers blurred across the keys: tiny demons filled with fire. Robby twisted his guitar and women-shaped melodies snaked from the speakers. John smashed his drums like a child smashing glass.

You don't know me, Jim thought. *You think you do, but—*

His left hand flexed, clutching the trembling stage. He closed his eyes and his mind buckled. Cold blood ran through his body. His back arched and he imagined a thick tail swishing behind him. The crowd roared like an ocean, his blue eyes snapped open (glowing yellow in his mind), and for one heartbeat the backs of his hands appeared covered with hard scales.

See me CHANGE, Jim thought. A trick of the stage lights, maybe. An effect of the acid, almost certainly. Either way, he licked his lips with a forked tongue and sprang to his feet. The band emerged seamlessly from their improvisation and, half-human/half-lizard, he slithered to the mic stand. Grasping it, he stood in the spotlight, clad in tight leather pants and Cuban-heeled boots, while the crowd's singular mouth rumbled. They cast their affection at him, and he reciprocated with his soul. He purred into the mic and his voice formed bridges. His eyes fluttered, blue again. Cool sweat glimmered on his throat. Jim sang the final verse and chorus of "The End," and then sank through their applause like a man wrapped in chains.

Midway through the encore—"When the Music's Over"—Jim noticed the raven. It circled above the crowd, sometimes swooping low, mostly riding the thermals of their energy. He should not have been able to see it: a black and heavy bird amid such darkness, but its silky feathers caught the glow of the stage lights, allowing him to discern it with ease. Indeed, it appeared to shimmer preternaturally, finding light where there was none. As Jim recited the poetry section of the song, he heard the raven caw—a discordant, brilliant sound that punctuated every verse. He followed its flight around the theater, thinking it should soon disappear (it wasn't real, after all, but surely another lysergic twist), but the raven proved pertinacious. Before the song's end it glided over Jim's head and alighted atop Ray's keyboard bass. The bird shook its dark feathers and looked at the singer. It cocked its head and blinked bright eyes. Ray continued to play, oblivious.

I need that bird, Jim thought. *I need to feel its feathers ... know that it's real.*

Distracted, Jim finished the number. The music ended and the lights went out. The raven shimmered and watched him.

Camera flashes and questions, hands touching him, too many people calling his name. The whole world was backstage. Reporters, VIPs, groupies, friends of friends, industry people, hangers-on, lackeys, and dogs. He was pulled in too many different directions, but went to none of them. At times like these Jim floated away:

Part-fantasy, part-memory. All-refuge. A highway in the desert, a tangle of metal, and a scatter of bleeding Indians. An accident ... he didn't know what had happened. He stood in the middle of the road and absorbed the chaos, listened to the screams. He turned his gaze to a dying man thrown to the side of the road, broken and bleeding. Jim's fragile heart drummed. The Indian looked at him....

"Jim ... Jim."

"What is 'The End' really about?"

"Your appearance last month on *The Ed Sullivan Show* caused—"

"What's your stand on the war in Vietnam?"

Jim watched the Indian die—saw the life flutter from his eyes. Fascinated, he stepped a little closer, and then witnessed something amazing: the Indian's soul, slithering from his broken body. It shimmered, moon-bright and lizard-shaped, and crawled toward the boy....

"Jim ... come on. Come with me, baby."

He recognized Pamela's voice and opened his eyes. She stood before him, protecting him from the barrage of senseless attention. His cosmic mate. His love. Her red hair burned and he touched it, and felt her in his fingertips.

"Hey, baby," he said.

She smiled. "Come with me, Jim."

He started to go with her, but paused. Beyond Pamela—beyond the swarm of people—the raven swooped and landed on a rail. It pecked its glowing feathers for a moment, and then looked at him.

I know what you are, Jim thought. *You flew from a broken body. You're someone's soul.*

"Are you okay, baby?" Pamela touched his face.

The raven cawed. It rapped on the rail with its bony beak.

"Gonna fly tonight," Jim said, speaking to Pamela but looking at the bird. "Real high. I may never come down."

She kissed the underside of his jaw. "Don't leave me, Jim," she said.

But he did leave; twenty-five minutes later he was walking the streets of Baltimore, having escaped the backstage madness. He told the guys that he was stepping outside for some fresh air—didn't mention that he was, in fact, following the raven.

An unusual fog draped across the city, in places so thick that Jim could hardly see an arm's length in front of him, and then it would dissipate and hang in smoky ribbons, coiled like snakes around the streetlights, whispering across his skin as he walked. The raven flew just ahead of him, moving from fencepost to trashcan to the hood of a parked car, and as Jim drew close it would ruffle its feathers and take wing again, leading him deeper into the night. He drew his collar tight and followed with his head down, eyes up. Cars hissed by, too close, too loud. Their headlights bullied the fog, revealing its seams.

Maybe none of this is real, Jim thought. *The raven, the fog, the cars. Maybe I'm still on stage, trapped in my haze while the band plays.*

It was cold, too, and the fog was heavy with moisture. It tasted like camphor. The city's light gave it a burned hue, and within it the raven shimmered, just like it had in the theater. There was no chance of him losing sight of it, even when the mist thickened; it glimmered, like the Indian's soul.

My soul, Jim thought, weaving slightly. His boot heels clicked rhythmically off the sidewalk. He heard car horns sounding, a train shuddering along the Northeast Corridor, and the raven's bruised cry, teasing him along.

He spared little thought for Pamela or the guys. They'd all be looking for him, no doubt checking the restrooms and darkened backstage areas, expecting to find him entertaining one of the many female partisans who had crashed the after-show parade. They would give up soon enough, if they hadn't already, conceding that he had gone AWOL, and not for the first time.

"Not for the last," Jim said. He smiled. The raven worked its wings and carried him away. He walked, listening to his boot heels, watching the raven. He had no idea where he was. Down alleyways and beneath trembling overpasses, across silent streets and through neighborhoods of old brick and faceless glass. He had lived in many cities across the United States—an unsettled upbringing; the eldest child of a Navy Admiral—and they all started to feel the same after a while. Climatically different, sure. Demographically diverse, certainly. But they shared a similar *feel*, he thought: just grids upon grids, filled with buildings and stoplights and authority, sustained by people who worked and ate and prayed and copulated: the great American prison. No wonder he continued to move around ... to slip through the bars and fly.

But this place, this town ... it felt different. Maybe it was the—
acid
—camphor-taste of the fog, or the kinked streets and heavy, ancient brickwork. Jim wasn't sure, but he knew he had never been any place like this before.
Where am I?
In reply, the raven uttered an abrasive cry, circling in the mist to alight upon a street sign. It was archaic in design: wrought iron, with gilded letters on a sooty background. Jim smiled when he read the sign.

"Yeah, pretty neat," he said, nodding. "Now I know this isn't real."

The raven snapped its fat wings and tapped its beak against the sign.

It read: Night's Plutonian Shore.

Strings of fog curled around the elaborate ironwork, and with a burst of angry sound the raven took flight, leaving a spray of black feathers that swayed to the damp sidewalk like burned leaves. The bird cawed, flickering in the mist, and then swept down, beneath a rustic archway and into a narrow alleyway. It flew ahead ... a glowing apparition in the distance.

Jim followed, boot heels clicking.

And the sound of his heels was soon enveloped by another sound, not dissimilar: the ticking of a clock, only it was loud—*too* loud, booming from within the confining alleyway, making the fog tremble and the old bricks shake in their joints. Jim covered his ears but, like the music when he had been lying on the stage, he could feel the thunderous ticking vibrate through the plates of his skull. He screamed, but could not match the sound.

The raven swooped and glittered ahead of him.

Death, Jim thought. *I can hear you. Tick-tock, my pretty child, my sweet one.*

He screamed again.

It grew darker, colder, narrower, as he stepped deeper into the alleyway. Soon all he could see was the fog and the raven, and he had to put his arms out to his sides to make sure that the walls were still there. The bricks were slick beneath his fingertips, like snakeskin, and they continued to quiver as the ticking sound crashed around him.

"What do you want?" Jim asked the raven. "Do you want my death? My broken body?"

He received no reply from the bird, which soared and, for a moment, flickered from view. Jim stopped and waited. Moisture gleamed on his brow and he drew his arms close to his body. He had never felt so alone. Five long seconds. A drifter on Night's Plutonian Shore. And then the raven reappeared with an almost musical swish of wings and Jim sighed, drawn toward it, walking quickly.

He could hear his boot heels again; the ticking had subdued to normal volume. Not that *any* aspect of this night could be considered normal.

I don't know what's going on, Jim thought. *But I have to see it through. I have—*

Something touched him in the darkness. It felt like fingertips brushing over his cheek. He cried out and stepped back, and a steely hand clasped his upper arm from somewhere else. Jim shook it loose, staggering slightly—felt someone else touch his face, and yet another hand reached out and grabbed the lapel of his leather jacket. He slapped it away, crying out again, shuffling down the alleyway as yet more hands poured from the darkness, each seeking some small part of him. He could hear voices, too, melding with the clip of his heels and that constant ticking: *Jim ... over here, Jim ... Jim ... look this way ... over here....* A sudden burst of light that he recognized as a camera flash. Jim shielded his eyes, but not before he saw what the alleyway had become: a jungle of hungry arms, bursting from the walls, hands snatching. *Jim ... right here, just one shot ... this way, Jim ... look....* Another camera flash. Hands grasped at him, fingernails raking down his leather pants, clawing his jacket. He could feel them in his hair, on his throat. He started to run, pushing the arms away as he hastened down the alleyway. His heart clamored in his chest and for the first time he felt afraid. He closed his eyes and the camera flashed again, urging its harsh glare against his eyelids. The silhouette of the raven—wings spread—was printed against the shocked membrane of skin.

Jim crouched, eyes closed, head down, and went to his refuge.

This memory/fantasy ... looking at the Indian's soul: a lizard-shaped thing of light, slithering across the blacktop. Jim watched it all the way, its tail swishing heavily, its

spines fully erect. He could hear, from amidst the chaos, a baby crying, and a young
man screaming. Blood ran across the highway and the morning sun painted every-
thing bronze.

Another camera flash, lighting the alleyway like fire. The hands continued to grab at him, but softer now, and fewer of them.

"And all my days are trances," a soft voice spoke from somewhere in the alley-way. "And all my nightly dreams/are where thy dark eye glances/and where thy footstep gleams."

Jim's heart ran harder, but he wasn't afraid. It was adrenaline, icy and crys-
talline—a sense that something life-altering was about to happen. He watched as
the soul-lizard crawled steadily toward him, its claws clacking and scratching on
the road. Would it simply disappear ... to the place where souls float freely? Jim
shook his head; he knew what was going to happen. The soul-lizard stopped a short
distance in front of him, lifted itself to its rear legs, and suddenly sprang. A cool flash
of light, and Jim felt it penetrate his vulnerable body. He held out his arms and stared
at the scrubbed blue sky.

CHANGE.

CHANGELING.

I am the Lizard King.

Jim stood and opened his eyes. No cameras, no grasping hands. It was, once again, an alleyway of old brickwork, flooded with lambent fog. The raven had disappeared, but ahead of him—not twenty feet away—glimmered a streetlight. Like the sign, it was archaic in design, emitting a plush yet tasteless glow. It was not, however, the streetlight that demanded Jim's attention, but rather the indi-vidual standing beneath it.

Jim blinked sweat from his eyes, took a deep breath, and started toward him.

"There is a gentleman," the individual said, "rather the worse for wear."

"I guess I was born that way," Jim said, drawing nearer.

The man laughed—a dry sound, like splitting wood. He was of slight build, with a wave of black hair and a full mustache. His eyes were dark, yet penetrative, sparkling beneath a well-formed brow, and his clothes were as old-fashioned as the streetlight he stood beneath. Jim—a disciple of the written word—knew exactly who he was.

"How shall the burial rite be read?" the slight man inquired. He pulled a watch from a pocket in his vest and flipped it open. The ticking sound grew loud again. Not booming, like before, but loud enough.

"The solemn song be sung?" Jim added.

The man nodded approvingly. "The requiem for the loveliest dead/that ever died so young?"

Jim took another step forward. "This is the craziest trip yet, man."

The man smiled and glanced at his watch. "A trip, you say?"

"Yeah ... I say."

"Do you know who I am?"

Jim laughed. His chest ached with the force of it. "Yeah, I know. You're the Acid Man, the King of Trips. Nothing more than a long, prolonged derangement of the senses, inviting me—as ever—to obtain the unknown."

"Am I real?"

"You're real in my head," Jim replied at once. "So yeah ... that makes you real."

"And if I were to inform you that I am real *outside* your head?"

"You're Edgar Allan Poe," Jim said, smiling. "You died in eighteen forty-something."

"Nine," Poe said.

"Yeah ... nine. You *can't* be real outside my head."

"But if I am?"

Jim smiled again, but his eyes dulled with uncertainty. "Then I would say that on this occasion ... I really *have* obtained the unknown."

"The unknown," Edgar Allan Poe said, and his dark eyes danced. "Welcome to my world, James."

"Oh the bells, bells, bells/what a tale their terror tells/of despair." Poe let the watch swing, pendulum-like, from its chain. "How they clash, and clang, and roar/what a horror they outpour...."

Jim cocked his head, listening to the watch's infinitesimal cogs strike unnatural sounds in the musty air. It sounded more like a heartbeat, he thought. His own, perhaps, thumping life into this esoteric body. He shuffled forward, standing now in the stale glow of the streetlight. A single glance upward, looking for the raven, expecting to see its ghostly radiance high above, like the moon behind cloud. But there was nothing. It was just him and the man.

Poe.

"Time is running slight," he said, snapping the watch closed and dropping it back into his vest pocket.

"Same for everyone," Jim said.

"But it ticks so loud for you," Poe said. "Jangling and wrangling. So close."

Jim raised one eyebrow. "Should I be afraid, Mr. Poe?"

"What is there to fear?"

"You tell me," Jim replied. "Your watch stopped ticking over a hundred years ago; I would expect you to have all the answers."

Poe nodded. He leaned against the streetlight, casting no shadow.

"We are very alike, James," he said. "Both of us flexing—raging—from our dark, internal corridors, largely condemned and misunderstood. We are children of arcane verse ... American poets."

"Why did you bring me here?"

Poe held out his hands. "You brought yourself."

"I followed your bird. Your soul."

"Drawn by the unknown ... testing reality."

"Why?"

"Because, like me, you're curious. You seek truths in untoward places." Poe pushed away from the streetlight. He took two silent steps toward Jim. The fog swirled around him—odd, dancing shapes. "I understand you, James, like no one else. I know how your mind works, and what you desire. We're quite the same, you see."

"Really?"

"Indeed. Like you, I'll always wander this dark path. I'll always be a word man."

"Better than a bird man," Jim said.

The fog curled and waned, and Jim could see, behind Poe, a wooden door. His mind continued its trickery; the door was not part of any building, or built into any wall, but stood alone, rather plain, appearing to hover in the thinning fog as if some divine brush had painted it into existence. Jim took a step toward it, half-smiling.

"What is this?" he asked.

Poe looked from Jim to the door, and then back to Jim. The watch thumped in his pocket, and Jim's heart kept time.

"The Door of Perception," Poe replied.

"I would think, Mr. Poe," Jim started, "that you could be more original."

"I may surprise you yet."

A legend had been inscribed upon the door—neat little letters. Jim had to step closer to read them:

> Who entereth herein, a conqueror hath bin;
> Who slayeth the dragon; the shield he shall win.

Jim felt a runnel of sweat trickle from his hairline, into the hollow of his cheek. He looked at Poe, searching his eyes for some suggestion of unreality— a frailty in the seams, perhaps, where imagination had hurriedly put him together. But Poe showed no such weaknesses; he appeared as real as anything Jim had seen.

I need to come down, Jim thought. *I need to escape.* He reached out and touched Poe, then turned and touched the door. Both solid. Both *there.*

The ticking sound continued to make the air shudder. Jim was no longer sure if it was the man's watch, or his heartbeat.

He touched the door again. "Where does it lead?"

"The Other Side," Poe said, smiling.

"Naturally."

"Time is running slight, James." Poe touched the door and with a childlike cry it swung inward. Jim's gaze was dragged to the opening: a rectangular rift in the fog. He could see nothing of the Other Side, only darkness: a bed of black fuel waiting to be ignited.

"It's a grave," Jim said. He tried to inch away but could not. "If I step through that doorway, all of this becomes real. I'll never wake up."

Poe raised his eyebrows. "How much of the unknown do you truly wish to obtain?"

"I'm not afraid." But his heartbeat suggested otherwise. Like the watch, it clashed and clanged and roared. Disorientation swept over him and he staggered either forward or backward, his legs buckling, the fog whirling in his brain. He remembered the arms that had thrust from the alleyway walls, and wished that he could feel them now. They would grab and scratch and make him bleed, but they would hold him upright and keep him from falling into that terrible doorway.

"Come, James," Poe said, stepping toward the darkness.

"I think I'll stay here," Jim said, trying to back away, but the doorway inched toward him. He turned around, his breath catching in his throat, and then the doorway shifted—to the side, and then in front of him again.

"Truths and answers abound." Poe's eyes glistened like the raven's feathers.

"I think I'll just wake up now."

"Come ..." And with a single step Poe disappeared into the darkness, leaving nothing but his voice, spiraling in the air, as thin as candle smoke: "Come ... follow me down."

Jim tried to—

WAKE UP

—convince himself that none of this was happening, and with the same mindspace he fought/thought to resist the doorway. But it *pulled* him, tempting, like a drug he had already taken. The more he struggled, the closer he got ... until finally, with his heart crashing and a terrible moan rising from his chest, he succumbed.

Darkness: a thousand nights crammed into one tiny space.

The door slammed closed.

Ladies and gentlemen ... from Los Angeles, California ... The Doors.

He heard the band's driving intro to "Break On Through" and stepped into the spotlight. The crowd erupted; he could feel the air trembling. Adoration, like a warm sheet falling over his cold body. *A pall,* he thought, trying to gaze beyond the stage lights, hoping to see their faces. They rippled and flapped and created such a frenzy of sound, but he could see only darkness. He slithered to the mic stand, as he always did, listing slightly, and prepared to sing the opening verse. The lyrics were ingrained in his mind, but the words that came from his mouth were all wrong: a deviant, broken, criss-cross of mad language. Nobody appeared to notice, however; the band continued to play, and the crowd kept cheering.

"The darkness in my temps âme/mort in le desert...."

Where's my head, man? This is wrong, all wrong—

He could hear ticking, thumping ... beyond the applause, the wild, flapping crowd.

"Beautreillis dreaming/L'enfant cries/le corbeau comes to eat my eyes...."

Jim screamed into the mic: a blistering torrent of bruised sound. It felt like he was chained to some crazy carnival ride, spinning and flashing while a calliope played. *Get me off this thing,* he thought. He tried to tilt out of the spotlight, but it followed him across the stage, as close as a tattoo. *Get me OFF.* The audience flapped their devotion, like the rumble following a thunderclap, and the band played on. Jim turned to them, confounded ... only to see a grotesquery so spectacular that all the strength deserted his legs. He fell to his knees—wanted to cry.

They played their instruments with notable gusto, with normal hands and bodies, but from the collars of their normal clothes sprouted oily, ravens' heads. Their beaks were long and black, and their round eyes glimmered in the stage lights.

I'm still tripping, Jim thought, getting slowly to his feet. *I didn't wake up, I'm still*—He turned again to the crowd and at that moment the house lights came on. The theater blazed and Jim could see everything: the main floor and balcony, the doors and walls and catwalks. And, of course, he could see his audience ... a million thunderous fans.

Not human—not even close.

Ravens packed the auditorium. The air was almost solid with them, bursting from their seats, scattering feathers, without room to fully work their wings, sinking down and bursting up again. They cawed and flapped, creating dissonance that sounded like riotous applause. And beyond this sound, beyond the music, he could still hear that ticking; that heartbeat.

Clash and clang and roar.

Jim held out his arms, shrieked, and ran to the edge of the stage. He threw himself off, and for a—

heartbeat

—moment thought he would fly, but then he was plummeting ... through feathers and beaks and claws. The theater floor opened up and he fell for too long. *So this is the Other Side,* he thought. *No one here gets out alive.* Laughter touched the edges of his scream, and just as he began to believe that he would fall forever, he landed in a twisted room of Poe's design, where the sound of his heartbeat shook the wooden floorboards, and where the raven was waiting.

"Four days prior to my death," the raven said, "I was found on a street here in Baltimore, in a most disheveled state. I was incoherent ... bewildered, having been missing for a number of days. Many questions were asked, not least of them how I came to be wearing somebody else's clothes. I was hastened to Washington College Hospital, where I regained consciousness only long enough to declare, 'Lord help my poor soul,' and then I passed into this otherworld ... Night's Plutonian Shore."

"Yeah, I remember reading about it," Jim said. "So much mystery surrounding your death. That's some way to go, man."

The raven nodded. It was perched upon a crooked tower of ancient books, among them Swedenborg's *Heaven and Hell,* Machiavelli's *Belphegor,* and Sir Launcelot Canning's *The Mad Trist.* Dust puffed rhythmically from between the dry pages as Jim's heartbeat rolled through the floorboards.

"My wife, Virginia, died," the raven said, "and my world turned to darkness. No—an unimaginable blackness. Take a knife to darkness, cut it, and it would bleed the stuff of my world. Of course I turned to the demon drink—prolonged my senses to obtain the unknown. I believed in a between-world wherein Virginia lay as pale as cloud, her eyes open, her sweet heart moving. I strived to reach this world by way of alcohol ... and sometimes I did; I held my dearest Virginia, in reverie, and my tears fell into her open eyes. Such ardor affects one's state of mind, and mine deteriorated quickly. My life was in pieces, and so I sought, in my delusion, to obtain another."

The raven flapped its wings. The tower of books creaked, and with a little snap of sound the bird hit the air, to alight, moments later, upon a bust of Pallas. Jim followed its short flight with glazed eyes. He sat against a stone wall and waited for this to be over.

Was there a quicker way out? Jim glanced around Poe's room. It was a grand space, confined by the detritus of creativity: the books and the bust, of course, along with crates and coffins that spewed exoticisms: an angel of the odd; the musings of Thingum Bob, Esq.; an oblong box; a loss of breath. The crates were stacked to the vaulted ceiling. There were window ledges, but no windows, only the shapes of windows carved into the stone. Likewise there was no door. The wooden floor ticked and thumped, and oval portraits (depicting yet more oddities) trembled on the walls.

No way out.

The raven rapped and tapped upon the bust, demanding Jim's attention.

"Thought I," it said, "that a man whose coat is worn and frayed will simply acquire a new one. Could the same not be done with a man's life ... to cast aside the cracked shell and inhabit one of fortitude? My diminished mind certainly believed so, and thus began my peculiar endeavor."

Jim looked at the shapes of the windows, seeking some seam of light, something he could rift. There was nothing. He studied the gaps between the floorboards, which sighed with every frantic crash of his heart.

Rap-tap upon the bust again.

The raven ruffled its feathers. "It was a desperate period for me—seeking a new body, one not so forlorn, so broken. For the simplest transition, I sought an individual not unlike myself, slightly younger, perhaps, but ablaze with the fire of creativity. In time I made the acquaintance of a brilliant young poet named Christopher Reynolds, and through wile, device, and dementia attempted to possess his physical form."

Jim looked at the raven. He imagined souls floating in the breeze, a glowing menagerie, seeking some warm place to land.

"You have to remember," said the raven, "that I was very sick ... confused."

"That's what happens when you crawl back in your brain," Jim said.

"For several days we struggled, clawing and biting. I assumed his clothing, but nothing more; Reynolds's soul was lion-shaped and it bested me. He threw me—shattered and delirious, still dressed in his clothes—to the cold streets. The fight was over; I had lost. My life was finished. In the passages of delirium before my final breath, I realized my mistake, and vowed that it would be different next time. 'Lord help my poor soul,' I uttered, and turned then to my raven form. And for these last one hundred and eighteen years I have flown Night's Plutonian Shore—an ancient lunatic—waiting for the right soul ... the right *poet* ... so that I might swoop and live again, young and beautiful, infinite with creativity, as dark as sin."

Jim tilted his head and blinked. His heart thumped harder.

"And here you are," the raven said.

"Except none of this is real," Jim said.

"If that's true, you have nothing to fear." The raven bristled, its feathers so slick they looked wet. "I'm taking your life, James. That's why you're here."

Jim got to his feet. He pushed away from the wall and took two sideways, unsteady steps. "You're just a dream. Or some freight train of hallucination barreling through my consciousness. I can't believe this is happening."

"Think of me as an angel," the raven said, "with wings where I had shoulders ..." It held up one talon. "... as smooth as these claws."

"I want to wake up now," Jim muttered.

The raven cawed and, once again, rapped its hooked beak upon the bust. Cracks appeared in Pallas's smooth white eyes. "I'll not make the same mistake again, James. The eyes, you see ... the eyes are the windows to the soul. This time I know the way in."

Jim shook his head and screamed.

WAKE UP!

"Be not afraid," the raven said, and Jim heard its wings snap at the air. "You don't want your life, anyway. Your audience—your world—is full of scavengers, tearing you to pieces. They don't understand you. *Nobody* understands you."

Jim remembered the grabbing arms and camera flashes. His heart slammed like an earthquake and he saw, in his mind's eye, his audience: a million frenzied birds, ready to claw.

"No," he said. His voice seemed far away.

Even the band ... different creatures.

I'm alone, he thought, and closed his eyes.

"From the thunder and the storm," the raven said. "And the cloud that took the form/(when the rest of Heaven was blue)/of a demon in my view."

Its wings made thunder, and all Jim saw was darkness.

Follow me down.

Dawn sun. A blind red eye, unblinking in the east. The smell of oil and sand and the sound of weeping ... of hurting. Jim stood among the chaos, naked, violated. Blood dried in the dead Indian's hair. His brown hands touched nothing. A breeze rippled his clothes. Jim felt the soul-lizard inside him, twisting like a child. He embraced it and kept it warm. NOW YOU'RE MINE AND I AM YOURS. *He felt the stroke of its tongue, the flick of its tail. The chaos made crazy shadows. Jim looked at his. It slithered and pulsed and Jim thought,* SEE ME CHANGE.

Time is running slight.
I understand you, James.
We're quite the same, you see.
Follow me down.

CHANGE.
CHANGELING.
It opened its eyes.
I am the Lizard King.

The lizard's blood ran cold and slick and angry. Its scales flushed with fresh color, and it squatted close to the trembling floor. The raven swept low and dragged its talons across the lizard's rigid back. The lizard hissed and flicked its tongue. It struck with one claw, but the raven was out of reach. It flapped its wings and ascended to the top of the book tower.

"I'll destroy your soul," said the bird. "I'll leave your body empty and gasping, and then I'll simply glide inside."

"And if my body dies?" the lizard said.

"It is young and strong," the raven replied. "And not ready for death."

"You should know I'm not afraid."

"The foolhardiness of youth." The raven shook its feathers. "You think you know darkness; you write songs about 'The End' ... but you know nothing. When you have lost the one thing you truly loved ... when the eye of madness glares long and hard upon you ... when shadows touch your every waking moment and fill your mind with screams ... only then will you know darkness. But you, lizard, are yet a shimmer; and I shall fill that beautiful body, and take it to incredible places."

With a passionate cry the raven took wing, rising from its perch and soaring toward the lizard. It extended its claws, screeching, wanting to strip its thorny skin. But the lizard flexed its spines and lashed forward with snapping jaws. They collided with harsh cries and an explosion of black feathers. The lizard felt its tough skin tear, its cold blood drip. It raked its claws across the raven's wing, shedding yet more feathers, and then the bird was rising again, to the lip of a crate, where it squawked and dragged its wounded wing.

The lizard showed its forked tongue. "You're going to have to do better than that."

The raven rapped and tapped in anger. "As will you, lizard."

And so began the clash of souls. No way to tell how long it lasted; no sense of night or day about the room—only the thud of Jim's heartbeat, running alternately fast and slow, connected to his soul as it fought, and then rested.

They attacked in spells, coming together in a mad and angry tangle. The lizard would clamp its jaws on the raven's wing, and the raven would gouge and peck, finding the soft flesh between its scales. They formed a new shape, a new monster: a lizard with wings; a raven with scales. This twisted creature would roll and scramble across the dusty floor, swishing its tail and spraying feathers, until—too exhausted to fight—it would separate to its component parts, blood-streaked and hurting, needing time to catch breath.

"You can't beat me, raven," the lizard said. Its yellow eyes flashed.

"Give me time." The raven's feathers dripped red. Its beak was notched and dull, like an old spearhead.

"You've had your time."

Another clash, squawking and crying. The raven covered the lizard's eyes with one wing and pecked at its unprotected stomach. The lizard twisted and whipped its tail, spines smashing against the bird's body. They rolled across the floor, scattering fragments of Poe's mind. The tower of books crumpled with a monstrous groan, old pages tearing loose and splashing across the floor. Crates toppled, spilling their arcane contents. Portraits were punched from the walls, and sagged in their cracked frames.

Puddles of blood. Two bruised, torn souls. The raven flapped with wounded wings to the lid of a split coffin. The lizard slithered into the shadow of an overturned crate and licked its broken scales.

"Almost over," the raven said. "Time is running slight."

The lizard trembled. How long had it been here, trapped in this fog-covered nightmare—this unforgiving trip? Days? Months? Its life before seemed like a long-ago thing. It recalled the baked earth of authority, and the cool nights of love. It recalled crawling into the public eye and seeing its blindness. Verses and choruses tumbled across its memory, as thin as matchsticks. Pamela's hair, smelling like smoke and honey, and the touch of her lips. Sleeping on rooftops and in the backs of cars. Mescaline and acid and the cold, constant drip of liquor. What was real? Could it be that the life it thought it had been living— the rock star, the poet, the Lizard King—had been an elaborate dream all along?

Had this dream stopped?

Jim's heartbeat drummed through the floorboards, but it was slower now. Weaker. *That's my body,* the lizard thought. *Slowly dying.* And with this realization came the knowledge that the heartbeat was the doorway. It was the *only* real thing. The only way out.

My heart. The lizard shifted its bleeding body. *My life.*

Beating slowly ... slowly.

The raven attacked again (motivated, also, by the rock star's dying body). It swooped with heavy black weight and sent the lizard spinning into one corner. It followed with its talons and beak, tearing the lizard's hard skin.

"His body is mine," the raven cried, blood dripping from its claws.

The lizard blinked its yellow eyes, puffed out its spines, and fought. Another long and wearing clash, entangled for hours, biting and scratching, lurching through the scattered ruins of Poe's mind. There came a final, fatigued flash of anger, and then the souls separated. The raven limped to its refuge and hid beneath one fractured wing, while the lizard pulled itself to the center of the room.

My heart, it thought.

The sound, now, was all too slow.

My life.

It was beneath the floorboards. Beneath this place of dark invention.

The only way out.

While the raven cowered and bled, the lizard gathered its remaining strength and, with claws flashing and tail slapping, assailed the trembling floor. It sought—as had been the case all night—the merest seam of unreality, and eventually found one: a crack in the floorboards, which with one hard lash of the tail became a split, and then a rift. The heartbeat grew louder, and cool blue light fanned from the wide seam. The lizard worked furiously, smashing and clawing great chunks of the floor away. The closer it got to—

life

—escape, the brighter the light became, the louder the heartbeat.

The raven fluttered from its perch and limped toward the lizard, dragging both wings. It screeched and showed its talons, defiant, but powerless. Its eyes were dull black stones and its feathers were crumpled. The lizard spared it a single glance, and then struck with its tail, connecting hard with the bird and flinging it across the room. It thudded against the wall, a broken thing. Blood-mottled feathers settled around it, as thick as oil.

The lizard roared—more lion than reptile—and clawed away a jagged section of floor. The light that erupted was geyser-like, rushing to the high ceiling, filling the room like music. The lizard had to turn away, momentarily blinded, and when it was able to look again it could see the source of that brilliant light.

His heartbeat. His life.

A door.

It shook in its frame as the life it knew—rock star, poet, and lover—pounded on the other side. And as the lizard crawled into the light and through the doorway, it heard two things clearly. The first was the raven:

"This is just the beginning," it squawked from its shattered place. "I will get you soon ... *soon* ... SOOOOOOOOOOOON."

The second sound was softer, kinder. The lizard clung to it as it fell through the doorway and into the light. Pamela's voice, like rain on piano strings.

"*Don't leave me, Jim*," she said, and the lizard closed its eyes—could feel her hair, and the sweet touch of her breath. "*Don't leave me.*"

He opened his eyes and looked, immediately, for the raven, but all he could see, blessedly, was Pamela's face. Her crystal eyes and freckled skin. She kissed him. One of her tears fell on his upper lip. He smiled and licked it away—thought for one moment that his tongue was forked.

"All right, all right," he said. "Pretty neat, pretty good."

Beyond Pamela, the Baltimore night was glittering black, skimmed with cloud. No fog. No raven. Jim sat up and Pamela kissed him again.

"We thought we'd lost you," she said. "We came out here looking for you, but you were nowhere to be found. We looked everywhere, and when we came out again ... there you were."

"I guess I was in the shadows," Jim said. He got to his feet, brushing grit from his leather pants. The rest of the Doors were there, clustered around the backstage entrance. They looked concerned ... frightened, even.

"One of these days, man," Ray said. "You're not going to wake up."

"I'll always wake up," Jim said. "I just don't know where."

He stepped away from them, leaning slightly to one side, his heels tapping on the ground. He could feel the lizard inside him, healing.

"Where are you going, man?"

Jim didn't answer. He kept walking.

Rue Beautreillis, Paris, France.
Saturday July 3, 1971.

The city slept, lights flickering like candles, with just a hint of violet dawn burning the horizon.

The raven alighted upon the balcony of the fourth-floor apartment, shook its slick black feathers, and waited.

The End, Beautiful Friend

Frankenbilly

By

John Shirley

O kay ... recording. I'm going to splice this with Henry's story, and make a whole presentation. I'm not sure if I can go ahead with my plans on it, though. I got a kind of warning today.

This recording is made on August 7, 1981. It's been, what now, about fifteen years since Henry came riding onto Corriganville, out in east Ventura County. What I'm going to remember for you now happened in 1966.

Now let me set the scene. It's the summer of '66, the day the rider comes, and we're shooting *Billy the Kid Versus Dracula* on the Corrigan Ranch. Me, I'm the soundman, hoping this is the last shot of the day. It's a damned hot day, even in late afternoon with the wind blowing in from the Mojave. My head throbs and my sweaty shirt rasps on my back as I adjust the boom mic over John Carradine and Harry Carey, Jr. Wishing I wasn't there at all. Getting paid barely enough money to make it worth showing up. But it's the only job I can get. Hell, the only job any of us could get.

Harry's playing a wagonmaster, Carradine is a vampire, and both are in costume, standing by a covered wagon, trying to catch some of its shade. "John," Harry says, "Why the hell are we in this crap picture?" Not much trying to keep his voice down.

Carradine just laughs affably, says in that voice that seems too deep for his skinny little body, "Because if we didn't we'd have to pursue honest labor, Harry."

Harry starts to answer back but then he shades his eyes with his hand and squints up at the hills over the movie ranch. "Looks like a rider up there, on top of that hill. Damn hot day to be riding out in the sticks."

Sounds like a line from a movie—a better one. I turn to look and yeah, there's a guy on a black-and-white pony up there raising some dust, moving his horse slow, watching us. I'm thinking it's one of the wranglers, probably, then get a funny feeling seeing him up there. The stranger's a long ways off. I can't make out his face, but I can feel him looking right at me.

Then the director shouts at me to get the goddamn duct tape slapped on the boom mic and get out of the way for the take.

Two and a half hours later the ordeal's over for now. No night shoot today. So I'm sitting at a card table set up by my little silver Airstream trailer, a hundred yards up-slope from the set, on the little dirt road that passes behind the "town." It's dusk, half an hour after we stopped shooting, trying to get the damned Revox reel-to-reel to stop jittering. Of course, we mainly did sound-to-film recording, but I'd been collecting some wild sound and atmosphere stuff for the foley editor to use later. And I'm listening to the crickets as the sun goes down, and fumbling with the reel-to-reel's switches—screwing up, because, to be honest, I'm drinking, right? More than usual, I mean. Been getting worse all year.

My wife ran off to Las Vegas with a broken-down stuntman, about a year before, took my savings with her. I'm forty-five years old and working on Poverty Row junk like this. My daughter hasn't spoken to me in almost a year, and I got fired off the last shoot for drinking.

Tequila. Maybe that's why Henry picked me. Or maybe he saw the stamp of destiny.

So I'm sitting in front of my Airstream, nursing my Cuervo, when I hear a clopping and catch this funny smell—not so funny, more like strange and sick. I look up from the recorder set up on the card table, and there's this leathery snaggletoothed rider squinting down at me from his horse. He's skinny, got jug ears and long gray hair. The sunset is in his eyes—blue eyes under heavy dark eyebrows. On his worn-out old saddle is a rifle holster, with what I assume is a prop Winchester in it.

I glance past him, see a trail of dust still hanging in the crotch between the scrubby hills. I figure this is the rider Harry spotted, the one watching us this afternoon. He's ridden down out of the eastern Santa Susana foothills around Corriganville. Old Crash Corrigan bought the ranch land back in the '30s and turned it into a low-budget movie set, mostly for Westerns and serials, but they made all kinds of pictures here, and parts of pictures. Even some Tarzan, and television, later.

But this rider, he's coming from the mountains—and on the other side of those mountains is the Mojave Desert. I figure he can't have come that far. Must be an extra fooling about with one of our rented horses, all afternoon. "If Mr. Beaudine sees you took one of our horses out for a joy ride," I advise him, "he's liable to fire your ass off the shoot."

"Don't know a Mr. Beaudine," he says to me. He had a voice that went from squeaky to gravelly in a few syllables. "Anyway, this here is my own damn horse. Pedro's his name."

"*Beaudine*'s his name—the director of the goddamn movie," I say. I remember trying to figure out how old the rider was—couldn't guess. Might be old or just weather-beaten, premature gray. I've never seen such leathery skin. Like it was stripped off, run through a tannery, and put back on. His hodgepodge outfit doesn't look like it belongs to the standard western costuming they put the cast in. He's wearing an antique military jacket—khaki, a few brass buttons left, yellow collar—like something one of the Rough Riders would have worn going up San Juan Hill. He has big dusty clodhopper boots on, dungarees, and a stained, dust-coated sombrero. There is a red bandana around his neck, though. That's the only bit of costumery on him that seems to go with the production.

He sits there, on one of those black-and-white Indian ponies, a grimy Pinto stallion who snorts and lowers his head to the ground, looking for something to crop up, but there's nothing but sage.

Music plays from one of the other trailers, a song by the Beatles. "Drive My Car." The rider looks toward the sound. "Now that's a queer song," he says. "'Beep beep beep,' they say." He sticks the tip of his tongue out to catch it between crooked buck teeth, as if to keep from laughing.

"That's the Beatles," I say.

"Sounds more like birds peepin' away," he says. "Say there, bub ..." And he leans over pommel of the most worn-out old saddle I've ever seen, to look real hard at the bottle of Cuervo sitting on the table. "That ta-keeler there?"

It takes me a moment to figure out he meant tequila. "Sure. Climb down and have a slug, bro." Anything to take my mind off my life....

He steps down off the horse, doesn't bother to tie it up. The Indian pony wanders off, and the rider doesn't seem worried about it. He limps energetically toward the other camp chair, sits with a grunt, slapping the dust off his dungarees. He accepts the bottle from me. "You ain't got a glass? I'm not barrel boarder. I'll have a glass if they is one."

"Sure...." I go into the trailer, find a second glass, and when I come out I see him poking at my tape recorder.

"Now don't touch that!" I tell him, sharply. "Not cool, man!"

He draws his hand back, sits up straight, shrugging, adjusting his bandana. "You use that machine to make a movie picture?"

"Just for certain kinds of sound effects. Here ..." I pour him the tequila.

He takes the tumbler and raises it to me. "Here's how!" He knocks back half a glass like nothing. He's real quiet for a minute, his face shaded by that dirty sombrero. "That's good ta-keeler," he says, at last. "Didn't drink much till ... after. What's your name, bub?"

"Jack," I tell him. "You?"

"Gone back to my own given name. Henry. Well, it was William Henry McCarty but I liked Henry."

I sit next to him. "You changed your name at some point, huh? Police trouble?"

"You could say. Started out, I went by Antrim, after my stepfather. He was a right son of a bitch. Never knew my real Pap. Later, when I got in some trouble for shooting that pig-snout Cahill, I went by Bonney. William H. Bonney." He smiles ruefully. "Alias Billy the Kid."

When he says that, I'm thinking, *Oh Jesus, we got a live one here. A grade-A liar or a grade-B lunatic.*

It's cooling off now, and he pushes his sombrero back so it hangs off his neck by the chin string. His hair's all tangled together. He goes on, "Got a cabin in southeast California, by the border now—and about twelve mile from my cabin, they got one of those places with the movie screens up so high. Folks drive their jalopies up to them, watch 'em outside. I can't get me a jalopy because I got no identity papers. So I take Pedro out and they let me sit on the ground by my horse and watch the pictures. They give me a little work, now and then. Pedro, I had him five years ... where's he gone to?" He looks around for the horse. "There he is. Don't wander off too far, Pedro.... What was we talking about?"

I'm guessing this is his idea of an audition. All "method" like, living the part. I pour myself a drink. "So you want to play Billy the Kid in this picture? They've cast that part already, Henry."

"Me? No, I'm too old to play ... the Kid." He grins, showing his crooked buckteeth. I'm thinking I've seen that face before, in a photo. He goes on, "But I expect I can be a help. Heard that Wyatt Earp got paid for talking about things." He spits in the dirt. "He advised on some Tom Mix movie picture. If that head-busting

Kansas cow-fucker could get the do-re-mi, why not me? I need some money for Doc Vic. Got to have some chemistry supplies."

"You want to be a consultant, you mean? Oh that's right ... you used to be William Bonney, alias Billy the Kid." I smirk and pour him another. Then it occurs to me that even though he left the Winchester on his horse, I ought to glance at him to see if he has a gun or knife or something, seeing as he's either half or whole cracked. I don't see a weapon, but one could be tucked under that old military coat. "Were you in the military?"

"No, I took this coat off a fella. He didn't need it no more. I just like the buttons."

He takes the refill in as dirty a hand as I've ever been around. And while I'm noticing this, I see a pale zigzag of scars all around his right wrist. Sewing marks, sutures, all laced up. There's something else odd about his hands but it takes me a bit to work it out. Then I get it: his right hand is larger and a bit darker than his left. His left is small as a boy's of maybe fourteen.

"You are looking at my sewin' scars," he says, frowning at me.

"Um—car accident?"

"Nope. Now, I heard that this here movie picture—" He pointed toward the production set, just visible between the old-timey false-front buildings of Main Street. "—is about Frankenstein and Jesse James. Now I didn't know Jessie but I know all about that German doctor. Much as a man can know about that one— he was not a man who showed his insides ... oh, here's how." He drains the rest of the tequila in his glass, *boom*, just like that.

"Wrong show," I tell him. "We'll be shooting *Jesse James Meets Frankenstein's Daughter* pretty soon, but this is *Billy the Kid Versus Dracula*."

"It's what? Guess I heard wrong then. I come too soon. This here's Corrigan Ranch?"

"This is it. And the picture we're doing now is *you* ... versus Dracula."

"Dracula, you say. I saw an old movie about him, back before pictures could talk. But he ain't real. Frankenstein, now, he was real—only that doctor's name's not Frankenstein. Howsomeever, I read that Miss Shelley's book. There's people say I cain't read. It ain't—it's not true. My Ma taught me, before the consumption took her. I read that *Ivanhoe* once. Most of it, anyway."

Henry seemed to be talking more to the setting sun than to me. He was staring unblinking right into it, over the top of the fake saloons on the dusty street Corrigan Ranch used for its cheap oaters.

"So Frankenstein was real, huh?" I said, sipping tequila, wanting to hear more of this fantasy. "That's far out." It'd make a great story to tell around the set, anyhow.

"That name Frankenstein was a lie Miss Shelley made up. A *book alias*, you might say. His name was Doctor Victor Von Gluckheim. Doc Vic, that's how I think of him—he knew that Miss Shelley and her friends, had 'em out to his castle in Austria. She was young, real young, then, no more'n eighteen. He showed her some things he was working on. Made a dead frog and a rabbit come alive, right in front of her. Showed her a dead man he bought, fella died in a lunatic house. Working on sewing that onto another fella, trying to revive 'em. He was in a struggle with death, don't you see. Was Doctor Vic told me this. Now, Doctor Vic was pretty old when I met him. 1881—more'n ninety years old. But he looked maybe sixty. He come over to this country back in 1816, running from trouble back home. Graverobbing charges, as you might expect. So he come out to hide in the territory where he could do his work in peace. I met him two days before Pat Garrett shot me."

I'm listening to him and sometimes I'm trying not to laugh and other times I stare at those mismatched hands and I wonder. My nephew George, in those days, worked for *Confidential* magazine. It occurs to me then that maybe there's some way I can get a story to sell him for *Confidential*. Something like, "'Billy the Krazed' Raids Movie Set." I'm testing the recorder anyway, so why not? "Billy the Kid—In His Own Words." Hell, I'd read it.

"Tell you what," I say. "You tell me how you met Frankenstein, or whatever he called himself, and I'll try to get you the consulting job. If you do get it, it won't pay much. Maybe we can do something with your story, anyhow. I could record it on this machine...."

Damn if his story couldn't be a movie itself. I think so now and I thought so even then.

Henry thinks about it and then he says real slow, "Maybe you're the one I saw in the dream."

"Which dream is that?"

"I had a dream that a fella would tell my story, my true story, but I had to ride the mountains to find him. Since my time with the doctor I've learned to take advice from dreams." He looks at me and says, real slow, "My story's been percolatin' in me many a year and it could be the time has come. I'll do 'er. One thing though—you got anything to eat, maybe some pork and beans? I like those canned pork and beans...."

"Got some canned chili. I'll get you some, but don't touch that machine."

So he eats some chili out of the can with a spoon, cold, really relishing it, his yellow teeth chewing with his mouth open. He seems to have some trouble swallowing, and drinks a lot of my jugged water to get it down. When he's done he asks, "You got a truck I see to tote this here modern trailer. I expect there's a battery in that truck? One of those big car batteries?"

"Sure. Why?" Is he thinking of stealing my truck battery? Maybe he's got a broken-down truck in the hills somewhere.

"I'll show you, by and by. Got a smoke, there, bub?"

Does he mean grass? "Lucky Strikes, if that's what you mean...."

"Now that's a name I like. Did some prospecting. Never had a lucky strike that wasn't a smoke."

I give him the pack and matches. He puffs the cigarette and drinks tequila and I switch on the tape recorder. What's coming up now is his voice, spliced in after my voice: Mr. William Henry McCarty aka Henry Antrim aka William H. Bonney—alias Billy the Kid.

There is a lot of lies told about me. One is that I'm left-handed. You can see I am no lefty. Another is that I was some kind of full-time cow thief. I threw a wide loop in my time but I'm no cow thief, or hardly ever. I was a good hand for Mr. Tunstall. It's true I did start out as a horse thief with ol' Johnny Mackie. Another lie is that I killed a man for each year of my life. Here's the truth on the Holy Book: I killed but nine fellas, before Pat shot me. After that, well....

See, bub, I was in Fort Sumner, in New Mexico Territory, visiting my girl Paulita. Her brother Pete was keeping a close watch on her. He didn't like a wanted man dating his sister.

We was to meet up in the cantina. I was playing cards that warm night, my back to the wall, watching the door for her, and for law dogs. I was a dozen hands into a game with a couple of vaqueros up from Old Mexico. I pretended to drink more ta-keeler than I was, letting them get good and drunk so they make all the wrong calls. Then into the cantina came this nervous, quick-walking old man with a big bush of white hair 'round his head and a beak of a nose. He wore a funny old gray suit and knickerbockers and he chewed a crooked cheroot. He spoke the Español to the bartender. Spoke it with a funny accent. "What the hell kinda Spanish that old duffer's talkin'?" I said it out loud in English, not thinking he'd understand me.

But he did. He turned, with his Spanish wine in his hand, and looked at me real close, raising one of those old spectacles on a stick to do it with; and he said in English, "I have learned my Spanish in Spain, young man. But me, I hail from Germany." He said it like, *Chermany.* "But I know many languages," says he. "Even some Comanche, I know." He looked me up and down and says, "I have not seen you here before...."

"You want to play some cards, old horse?" I ask him. "I'll take German gold same as any other."

When he smiled, there were only a few teeth in there. "No, I think not. You are an interesting young man. You have the stamp of destiny on you. Such I have learned to see."

That's how he talked. *"Such I have learned to see."* Struck me as real entertaining. A man sure gets tired of vaqueros and blacksmiths and cowpunchers for company. Here was a man who'd traveled to Europe. My Ma, she was born in Ireland, and I was born in New York, and I hankered to see more of the world. Especially when my neck was like to be fitted for a rope halter in New Mexico.

"The stamp of destiny," I repeated. "I like that."

He nodded and drank his wine, staring at me the whole time, then he gave me a little bow, from the waist, and walked out of the cantina.

"Well, I'll be goddamned," I said, and the bartender laughed.

"The doctor, Señor Victor, he has a silver mine," said the bartender. "But with no silver in it."

He told me the doctor had a cabin at an old silver mine that was all played out, some miles from town. He had some way to make ice down in that mine, where it was cool, and sometimes he sold it to the town. He did some doctoring on 'em too but most were scared of him.

"But he always smiles, and speaks softly to me." There was a priest, there, in the cantina, as drunk as any one of us, hearing me and the bartender talking, and he spoke up. He said, in Español, "The devil always wears a smile, and speaks with a soft voice."

I put it out of my mind and set to playing stud. That ricket-legged little Mexican dealing had given me three aces down. He was grinning, thinking he had me with his two pair, and his tall, drunken partner with the pitted face was trying to look all cucumber-cool so I knew he had a hand too. So I said, "Boys, let's bet it all out there, and see what happens."

They went for it and when the next cards were dealt I had me a full house, aces full of tens. When we turned those cards over I never saw two sicker-looking vaqueros. I scooped up the double eagles, except for one to buy 'em enough a drink or two, gave 'em a wink to go with it, and walked out. I was tired of waiting for Paulita—I was going to take the bull by the horns and find her.

I went out to my mare and was leading her out through another alley to the street, thinking about where I'd look for Paulita, when I heard a scuffling behind me. I knew right away what it was—the drunk vaqueros wanting their money back. I jerked my single-action and turned. Sure enough, they were coming out into the moonlight, side by side, the tall one unlimbering an embossed-silver shotgun while Mr. Rickety-legs was aiming his pistol. The pock-faced bastard fired and missed so wide I never even heard the bullet pass. Hell, he didn't even hit my horse. I couldn't hardly miss him from eight paces, and my first round caught him right in the middle of the chest, knocked him back off his feet. The other vaquero would have done for me with that shotgun but the damn fool hadn't cocked it. He was working on that, cussin' to himself as he realized it wasn't set, when I shot him through the throat, just above the collarbone—that'd be right there on you, bub. And over he goes, crying out "Madre Mia" and then spitting blood. He rolled over, tried to crawl away. I spent two more bullets making sure of them—and then I knew someone was watching. I could feel it.

I looked around to see a shadow shaped like a man out on the street, standing by a buckboard. There was a big halo, like, of white around its head. Then I worked out it was that German doctor with the light from the whorehouse behind him. He said to me, "Ach, hold your fire! The law will be here, chure—but if you help me load these men on my wagon, I'll tell them you were not here. And I will pay you for your help. You have already helped me much tonight."

He held up a little leather sack and jingled it. What did he mean, I'd helped him? Then I remembered that doctors liked to cut open dead folks to see what made 'em tick—and what made 'em stop ticking. And this man, something about him seemed like a kindly old uncle. Never had me a kindly old nobody. So I said, "You can keep your gold, I'm flush now. Come ahead."

We dragged the bodies to the buckboard, heaved them on. I heard some shouting, someone asking for the constabulary, the voices of the whores talking in Spanish nearby, so as soon as he got up on the buckboard I slapped his horse's rump and it pulled him off into the night.

Pretty sharp after that I rode off to Paulita's cabin, out on the edge of Pete Maxwell's ranchland. We were shacked up for true, hardly going out, for two days.

Well sir, we were drinking and lovin' up in that shack on a hot July night, not so different from this one, bub. But hotter, it was, hotter'n a whorehouse on nickel night. We got hungry, as you do. I thought I'd go to her brother Pete's house, cut some beef from his stores like he'd offered, maybe have a drink and talk to him about Paulita. Clear the air. We used to be friends.

I had no shirt on that night, just some jeans. No gun, because I didn't want to spook Pete. Just a knife in my hand for cutting some steak for me and Paulita. I rode over, barefoot and bare-chested, singing to myself. I was a pretty good tenor, you know. Hard to believe, hearing me now.

I was drunk but able to sit a horse, still remember that the air felt good on my skin as I rode. I reined in when I saw some strangers on the porch of Pete's place. I was wanted for shotgunning Bob Olinger and shooting one or two others, so I was nervous. I skirted around to the back, dismounted, and went in the back way, carrying that knife. Went to Pete's room to ask him who those fellas were on the front porch—couple of deputies, is who they were, I found out later—and then I see someone in there, just the shape of him in the dark. Doesn't look like Pete to me. So I say, "Quien es?" and *boom*, the fella shoots me. When his six gun goes off, that flash showed his face. Pat Garrett. I'll never forget it. Fella I'd ridden with, turned sheriff. He looked scared as a deer in a ring of wolves, even though he was facing a man without a gun.

He fired twice. One round went through my right hand, changed direction when it smashed a bone, passed through and smacked into my left leg right above the kneecap. Second shot cut into my chest. I guess it nicked an artery, and spilled a mess of blood into my lungs. Getting shot like that felt like being kicked by the meanest mule ever was.

Then I was flat on my back, trying to breathe, and Pat was yelling to his men, "I shot Billy, by God!" And there were a lot of voices, including Pete's. Then I thought: I expect I'm dying. Everything went black.

Next thing I remember is a stroke of lightning against the blackness. The blaze of the thunderbolt seemed to linger there, not going away like lightning usually does.

Second thing I remember is a voice speaking in foreign, like a man muttering to himself. I tried to open my eyes but they were too heavy. "Mr. Bonney, you are stirring, I see," he said to me. "Das ist gut. But now, sleep...."

After that, I remember the pain of sitting up. It never hurt so much to sit up, bub. The light hurt my eyes at first, too. Even though it was just a railroad lantern, down in a dark hole in the ground. Doc Vic had him a little operating room way down in that played-out silver mine of his. There was what looked like telegraph wires on the ceiling, nailed to the rafters, and there was a machine, big as a pedal sewing machine, 'cept it had a crank on it. Doctor Vic was turning the crank, faster and faster, and I felt right then like someone poured pure grain alcohol in my veins and lit it on fire. Soon after I went under again.

Next time I woke I felt some better. Just kind of funny. Like part of my body was missing, or half missing.

Something else was missing. I couldn't remember my name. Or who I was. Took me a long time to get that back. Years. It was in there somewhere, but locked away. Doc Vic said it was something to do with my poor brain losing breathing-air when Pat killed me.

Pat Garrett did kill me, too. The doc told me he bribed the Mexican fellas watching my body, replaced it in the coffin with one of the vaqueros I shot, or part of him. The doc drug my body back to his mine, covered in sawdust and laying on blocks of ice. He took it down deep underground, patched it up and he put the life back in it. He says my spirit was hanging around my body, like they do for a time after dying. When he called down the lightning for me it's like my spirit rode that lightning down—like a bronc-buster riding a thunderbolt. Rode it right back into ... up here. My brain.

I realized, when I woke up, that I was nekkid as a jaybird. This did not sit well with me. I was cold, and felt like a man with his back to the door on a night when his enemy is looking for him. But what bothered me more was all that sewing. My right wrist was sewed up. And my hand looked all wrong. That's because it wasn't my hand—Pat Garrett fair destroyed that hand—and this one belonged to that pock-marked vaquero I killed. You can see it's too big for me. My left leg from the thigh down belonged to that other hombre. It's crooked and fat, but I make do with it. Now, some of my inner parts is theirs too. I got my own heart, thank God, but my lungs belongs to the tall vaquero. Later I got me a new liver— a young priest died from falling off a horse, and the doc sent me to dig up the body. Hadn't been embalmed—liver was still good, he said. It was in winter, too, that helped keep it fresh.

Doctor wouldn't take body parts from people who died of disease on account of they was tainted. He liked to get the bodies of folks been killed from falls or hangings—or from being murdered, long as it wasn't poison. That's why he kept watch on me that night. Said he knew I was a killer the minute he laid eyes on me. Knew I'd tangle with those Mexicans. He saw the stamp of destiny on me, and he saw their destinies too—short.

How'd he do that? He spoke of the power of lightning and "animal magnetism." That thunderbolt power he put in me—he put it in himself. Not quite the same. He takes his different, in something he calls a charged tonic. He says that's because he never died. But me, I got to have it right in the old nerves. Now I got what he calls a feeder, right here in the back of my neck, just under my collar.

Me and him, though, we had one thing in common. The thunderbolt, it changed us both somehow. It makes a man live longer. Real long. And it makes him sense things, like a rattler sensing your footstep a ways off with his tongue on the rock.

When I woke up in that mine, he called me Billy and that sounded right. I had a few memories of my mother coughing her life away in a bed; of pulling hand-cuffs off my hands, seeing as the cuffs was too big for them; of seeing a pal gunned down. But I couldn't connect none of it. Seemed like it all happened to someone else. And when Doc Vic saw I couldn't remember much, he said he'd take care of me. "In essence," said he, "I am your father."

Now that made me feel good. I couldn't remember much of my past but there was something in me longing for a father. I guess it had always been there. So I went right along with that.

And I served that man for more than twenty-five years. That's right. For twenty-five years I never ventured far in daytime. Only at night.

One hot day, a diamondback twice as long as your arm came into the mine and reared up, hissing and rattling. That thunderbolt the doc put in me came flashing up so I was faster than the rattlesnake. It struck at me but I caught it right under its jaws—caught him a whisper away from my neck. I could feel his tongue tasting the skin on my throat. I held him out at arm's length and sent that lightning through my hands to him and that ol' snake just went rigid as a pine branch and started smoking. I burned his golden eyes right out of his head. We ate cooked rattler that night—cooked then and there.

Most of the time we stayed up north, out east of Fort Sumner, at the mine where Doc Vic poked and prodded me and made notes. He had a feud with Old Mister Death himself, so he kept on with his work to build other fellas up out of nothing but spare parts, like in that Mary Shelley book. He got one of them up and moving too, but that patchwork fella was an imbecile and mostly drooled and played with his private parts. One day he just keeled over dead.

I did errands and I dug in the mine and gave the silver to Doc Vic. It was mostly played out but there was a little silver to be found. And we still sold ice to the town, now and then. Time passed full queer for me in those days, and years went by like weeks.

One time an outsider came snooping around, knowing the old doctor had gold. This poor excuse for a road agent was a red-headed son of a whore with a scraggly beard and an eye-patch. I smelled him before I saw him—my senses was that acute, and Lord knows he smelled high. I came out of the mine, sniffing the air, that evening and then seen him ride up on a bent-backed hammerhead roan, and I said, "Smelled you coming, bub. What you want here?"

Gingerhead cleared his throat and he said back, "Your money or your life." He waved a rusty old pistol I doubt would have fired anyhow. "Bring that old fool out and I better see his gold. I've got a short-fused stick of dynamite in my saddlebag and I'll set it burnin' an' chuck 'er in the mine unless I see gold fair quick. Silver'll do, too."

"Sure, bub!" I said, grinning like I was simpleminded. "I'll do that!" And as I said it I walked up to his horse. "Let me just help you down, there, you can come and get the gold."

I knew he wouldn't go for that but it confused him a moment or two, and that gave me time to step close. I grabbed his belt and dragged him down off his horse, and threw him on the ground. To me he was light as a half-empty feed sack. I stepped on his gun hand, and while he was blinkin' his good eye and cursing, I took the gun and tossed it in the brush. Then I knelt down, put my hand on his neck and let go some of the thunderbolt, sent it burning into him, just like that rattler. Boom, he went stiff, his remaining eye popping halfway out. I started in to choking him and he couldn't fight, being all stiff with the electricity.

I killed him quick and good, drug him off to the mine, where the doctor praised me, and chopped him up for parts.

Now, you notice I don't carry a gun. That vaquero couldn't shoot straight and I got his hand. I can manage a Winchester if I have time to aim, is all. And anyway I don't need a gun so much now, with the thunderbolt in me.

Now at that time, more than twenty years after Pat shot me, my brain was finally mending. Killing this gingerheaded fella seemed to wake something up in me. Made me want to go sniffing around the world.

So the next night, when the doc was resting, I came out of the mine—and I smelled something in the air. It was perfume, wafting from the town though it was some miles off. It seemed to call to me. So I lit out, not even understanding what I was doing, headed into Fort Sumner. It was a full moon, like the night I met the doc, and I heard the sound of a piano from the cantina. I was starting to remember cantinas, and a few other things, like the women you find in them. I had my charge that morning, and still felt strong from it. If a man doesn't exert himself too much, why, a charge'll last a good three days—but it's when you first get it that you feel like you could take on an Army and laugh.

When I got near the cantina out comes a young fella dressed like a Spanish rancher, and walking like he's had too much ta-keeler. I stared and stared at him. I thought for a moment that it was me.

He looked a hell of a lot like I did when I was young. The young fella took no notice, just kind of weaving off down the street.

In a doorway next to the cantina there was an old barefoot peon in a sombrero, a gent we sometimes bought grub from. I asked him in Español, "Who's that fella?"

Said he, "That's Señor Telesfor Jaramillo." I asked him who this Telesfor's mama was. I didn't know why I asked—but somewhere in me, I was starting to remember things.

He tells me, "His mother was Paulita Jaramillo. She married Señor Jaramillo and this child came soon after." He grinned in a way that told me it was too soon after. Then he came over all solemn. "But she has died now...."

I felt struck by lightning of a different kind then. Paulita dead, and a child born to her—a grown child who looked like me. All of a sudden I had a fierce headache, and I had to sit down, right there on the road, because of what was coming back to me. I was hammered down by a hailstorm of pictures in my mind.

Telesfor Jaramillo. He had to be my son with Paulita. And then I remembered who Telesfor's father truly was—remembered all about myself. William Henry McCarty. Alias William Bonney. Alias Billy the Kid.

Now, I had no real fear anyone in town would recognize me. It was more than twenty years, and I looked a helluva lot different anyhow. My skin—well you can see for yourself. The doc had dipped me in some kind of preserving tonic when he first brought me to the mine, and it still shows.

I thought of going after that young man, telling him who I was—but I could not tell him *what* I was.

He believed he was the son of this Señor Jaramillo. It was better he went on believing that. Because I was a kind of half man, and half corpse. I could not bear for him to know what I was—and I could not lie to him.

Bub, I felt like my heart had been dropped down a deep cold well.

I determined to leave Fort Sumner. I could not be so close to my son and never speak to him.

I am ashamed to say I scarcely gave a thought to old Doc Victor. He had plenty of his charged tonic to hand—but I should have stayed with him, for he'd been poorly. I just stood up, there in the street, and walked to the livery stable. I had some gold on me, which the doctor give me for emergencies. I would make my way. I would be weaker without the thunderbolt cranker—but surely I could live without it....

I found an old man working at the livery and bought him tequila to get some questions answered. I found out there was no use going after Pete Maxwell, who betrayed me to the law—he died in 1898, and was beyond my reach.

But I could get to Pat Garrett, for he was known to be alive and well.

I bought a horse and saddle and I rode out to find Pat.

Everyone knew about Sheriff Garrett; they all knew he had killed Billy the Kid and was damned proud of it. Crowed about it in a book.

Ol' Pat was still in New Mexico—had him a ranch in the San Andres Mountains. I set to finding his place, asked around in those hills, saying I wanted work with him. Couple of cowpunchers pointed me to his place.

When I got close, I climbed a bluff that looked down on Pat's layout, spying it out. I was laying there, flattened down and admiring his herd of quarterhorses, trying to decide how I'd kill him—when I started to feel real weak. I ate some jerky and the food helped, but not enough.

Then I knew—it was the thunderbolt. It seemed I needed it to live on, after all. Maybe it was a kind of addiction. I'd never been so long away from the cranker, and hadn't counted on the exertion. Seemed three days was all a charge was good for.

I had to ride hard to get back home. Killed my horse just getting there. I made it into the mine, staggering by the time I got to the cranker and got my thunderbolt into me.

I reckon I had come back looking sickly, but Doc Vic didn't look much better than me. He was laid out flat on his back in the lowest chamber of the mine. He had been slowing down some—age finally catching up. He didn't say so, but I worked out that my being gone for three days had kind of knocked his pins out from under him. Doc was powerful attached to me. The son he never had, is what I was. I knew just how he felt, for I had to let go of my own son.

Laying there on his cot, he took my hand, smiling real sad, and said that he needed to go to sleep and kind of die, for a while—but he wouldn't be thorough-going dead. He would build himself up, from inside, only it would take time, a long time.

He closed his eyes, and asked me to lay him out on the ice we kept in the mine. He'd go into the long sleep there, and it'd take care of him.

I will tell you straight, bub, it made me weep like a woman when he said that. He was the only father I'd ever known. I was to be alone in the world again. And I'd run out and left him to fend for himself when he was feeling low.

So I gave him the tonic he kept ready for this long sleep, and he drank it right down—and went stiff as a board. But I could feel through the "animal magnetism" and all—he was still there. Every so often, his heart beat, just one little thump ... and a little while later, another.

I wrapped him up good, like he told me, in some medicine-soaked bandages. Then I went about my business. I had some of Doc's gold and silver—and I had the buckboard and a couple of horses. I put the cranking thunderbolt machine in the buckboard, then I rode out.

I thought about shooting down old Pat on my own, face to face. Wouldn't that have given him a turn, seeing me a short breath before he died? But there was a long memory in New Mexico about Billy the Kid. It concerned me. I had a horror of having people look at me and laugh at the patchwork Billy I was now. Then too, the habits of staying hid had gotten strong with me. I was Billy, but I was also a man who'd spent most of twenty-five years in an old silver mine. No, I had to do for Pat Garrett from a good distance. Keep Billy the Kid out of it.

So I played the harmless old saddletramp, and asked around about Pat's doings. I found that folks around about there had no great affection for him and his bad temper, especially a onetime cowboy turned goat rancher, a hardbitten red-faced young fella name of Jesse Wayne Brazel. Pat was always shouting at Brazel to keep his goddamn goats off his land.

I went to Brazel, and played some cards with him—and made sure I lost. This will sometimes make a foolish man trust you. Then we talked about his troubles with the old sheriff—and I allowed as how I had a reason to hate Garrett too. I told him real quiet that if he'd kill Pat, I'd pay him for it—and I'd pay some "witnesses" to lie and say it was self-defense.

Brazel said he knew a notorious killer name of Jim Miller who might do it. I said I'd pay him, or Miller—whoever did it. And I'd bribe up some witnesses. Jesse Wayne Brazel agreed.

I kept watch on the road betwixt Brazel's land and Pat's, from up in the hills. I had a spyglass and everything. It was cold up there, at my little camp in the boulders, just fifty yards over that road. Hell, it was February. But I didn't feel the cold so much—maybe if you've been dead, you're too well acquainted with the cold to be offended by it. The wind was singing a song and nipping my ears when two days later, I spotted Jesse Brazel, on the red dirt road down below, riding along one way, with his friend Print Rhode, and they come across Pat riding along in a buggy the other way, off to town. Pat was riding with a man named Adamson. Brazel stopped him and they argued, probably about those goats eating up all the grass Pat wanted for his quarterhorses.

I watched close, grinning to myself, that spyglass pressed hard to my eye. I saw it all.

I saw Pat Garrett get out of the buggy to relieve himself, pissing off the trail, steam rising up from the puddle. He was still talking, real loud and sharp, the whole time he was peeing—I could make out a word or two about property lines.

Pat was half turned away and Brazel and Rhode saw their chance. Brazel nudged Print Rhode, who stepped up to Pat, pulled a pistol, and shot him in the head. Pat fell dead in midstream, wetting himself on the trail. I was sorry I couldn't be there for him to see who done it to him. But I felt the satisfaction of it all the same, better'n a good meal after a hard ride. I had finished Pat Garret—and got it done safely.

Later, with me spreading around the gold, it was fixed up that it was self-defense, that Pat was going for the shotgun in his buggy. A fine lie it was too, and it protected me from being found out. No one knew Billy the Kid was still alive, and that he'd worked it to have Pat Garrett killed—for killing Billy the Kid.

But that feeling of satisfaction dried up quick as a waterhole in the August sun. A few days later, I watched from afar as the pallbearers put Pat in the ground—and soon's they were gone from Boot Hill, and the colored fella with the shovel had finished and gone home, down I went to the cemetery. I was all charged up with thunderbolt, and dug Pat right up. I pried open the coffin, hunkered down, put my hand on his chest, and shot the thunderbolt right into him. It made his eyes snap open so the coins flew off. His eyes kinda swiveled about in their sockets—he almost seemed to see me. 'Course, his brains was shot through and he was decayed some, but there was a spark hanging around him and I felt like he knew me, for a moment. "I just wanted to say howdy to you, Pat," I told him. "Wondering if you're enjoying your new digs. I put you here myself, Pat. It was me! I sure hope you can hear me." His mouth opened a little, and a worm crawled out and I could see the worm was glowing from the thunderbolt. Pat made a rattling sound, like he was trying to talk—and his eyes looked in two different directions. One of those eyes was smoking—and it sizzled away to nothing. I tried to jolt him awake again ... but he was gone. Still—that's what I call shaking the last drop from the bottle. I filled in the grave, hoping he could feel it, and made my way from there, back to the buckboard, feeling more revenged.

The bribes I paid the witnesses cost me the last of my gold. I went back to the mine, and checked on Doc Victor. He was the same as before, half dead and half asleep, all wrapped up on the ice. I toted him out, and a load of ice, and then I sealed the mine behind us, blowing up the entrance.

Traveling by night I took ol' Doc Vic and the thunderbolt cranker in the buckboard, cooled with ice.

I was set on seeing California. I had time.

Time's mostly all I've had since, bub. I found a spot to rest myself in the Mojave, out in the brush, and mostly I've been out there since. I put Doc Vic down in another old mine close by my cabin.

By day I do odd jobs. Sometimes I crank up my machine. I keep it in repair. And I find other ways to get a charge. Which reminds me....

That is the end of Billy's recording. But I'll tell you what happens next.

It's getting dark, as the tape runs out. Billy clears his throat, spits, drinks some tequila, then suddenly stands up and limps toward my truck, on the other side of the trailer. I follow after him, wondering what he's up to. He doesn't even ask my permission—singing "Buffalo Gals" to himself, he lifts up the hood of the truck. Propping up the hood, he turns to me and says, "I expect you think all this I told you is the biggest goddamn lie you ever heard. And maybe my hand was sewn up on the wrist by a regular surgeon. Well, have a look at this."

Then he takes off that red bandana and turns his back to the truck. That's when I can see a copper wire sticking out the back of his neck, at the top of his spine. It's a bit blackened and slightly melty, but solid enough. He takes a coil of wire from his pocket, twists it onto that piece of metal sticking out of his neck and fixes the other end on the truck battery. He fiddles with it—and then *crack!*, there's a spurt of electricity. I jump back, startled. I smell ozone and burnt flesh and I see him go rigid, grinning real horribly, standing there shaking like a preacher with his pants down.

Then it stops. The battery is drained. He's panting. He jerks the wire loose, and shakes himself, shivering and grinning. He coils up the extra wire, his eyes real bright. A wisp of smoke rises up from the back of his neck. It's getting darker out there by the second—but I can see him clearly, because there's some shine coming off him. His buckteeth are glowing and the whites of his eyes are sparkling with energy.

"I come a ways from my thunderbolt cranker," he says, his voice rough and strong. "I needed that jolt." I don't like the way he's looking at me. He goes on, "I'm thinking about your voice machine—that's the one got me worried. I put my story on there. I come here because I need some money. But there won't be any money, not real soon, ain't that right?"

"Would take a while, yeah. Maybe I can sell this story of yours or ..."

"No, no, you can't do that. I changed my mind on it. When I ponder it—why, it's not safe for me. It's not what was in my dream. I'll find some other way to get the money I need. I got to buy supplies, to help Doc. He's coming back to life, but he's still mighty weak. That recording thing won't be of any help any time soon." He paused, and rubbed a thumb and forefinger together thoughtfully, watching the sparks that crackled between them. "Howsomeever, it's good I set it down, for my story's told on there—and that's enough. Someday I'll give it to folks, but not yet.... Anyhow, bub, I'm going to take that roll of talk with me."

"The hell you are," I say sharply. "That tape belongs to me!"

He's still got that charged-up bucktoothed wolf grin on him. It's making me sick to look at it. He steps toward me. "I was afraid I'd have to kill you. And here we is...."

Billy reaches out his hand toward my neck. Electricity crackles blue and yellow between his fingers.

But the Corriganville security guard, Carlos, is coming along behind the buildings below us, flashlight in his hand. "Carlos!" I yell, backing away from Billy. "Need help up here! Intruder's trying to rob me!"

Carlos comes waddling up the slope, shouting, pulling his gun. He's a fat man and doesn't move too fast. But Billy doesn't like the look of that uniform and pistol. He hesitates now, eyeing Carlos—and I take that chance to run back to the Revox. I pull the tape reel off the machine and toss it into the back of the trailer. Then I lock the Airstream up and I toss the key far away into the darkness. Figure I'll get a locksmith later, or just bust down the door myself.

I turn around—and there is Billy, faintly glowing against the dimness. His eyes are sparking with anger and he's reaching for me—and there's a flash.

Then I am shaking on the ground. I'm not hurt too bad—mostly just stunned. Billy stands over me like he's going to finish me.

But Carlos fires a warning shot as he gets to the road and Billy is slipping around the other side of the trailer. I hear him whistling for Pedro and then I hear hoofbeats—and Billy the Kid is riding away.

I leave the area, soon as I get my truck battery charged. I head up to Northern California. Scared, but not ready to give up that tape. Might have done something with it, too, like write that screenplay—but I slide right into the bottle and mostly forget about the tape. I lose my house and my truck to drink.

I hit a bottom, deep down.

Then I find my way to AA—and I'm six years sober now. Working for a cable company, still living alone in my old Airstream. Thinking about that screenplay I'm not writing.

But this morning, I see a strange young woman standing out by my mailbox. She's wearing a camouflage-type military tee shirt and jeans. She's got almost no chin to her; she's tanned real dark and has her hair tied back in a dirty ponytail. I step out of the trailer, and she says to me, "Billy sent us to tell you, you're to give up the tape. His mind has found you, Jack, and you cannot hide now. He said to tell you and now you've been told. You get the tape ready, in a box, and we will come for it."

Then she gets in a dusty old Chevrolet, and it rumbles off.

That makes me remember a newspaper article from about two months ago. I saved it, pretty sure who they were talking about....

So I go into the Airstream and dig the clipping out of a junk drawer and read it again. And now I'm thinking that when I'm done with this recording, I'm going to go to the newspaper reporter who wrote this, and play this recording for him. I'll sell it all to him. Someone needs to know. Okay—I'll read that clipping out loud now:

> (Mojave Desert News) Reports that an unusual clan of religious devotees has taken root in the Southeastern Mojave have been confirmed by the Caliente Sheriff's Department. A number of complaints have been registered with the sheriff about the group, which is called "Children of the Thunderbolt." Residents in the area complain of late-night intrusions onto private land. There have been allegations the group has raided graves of the recently interred. Sheriff LeCoste has said the organization seems to be a "cult" that centers on the worship of a very old man, who is in a coma underground. The cult is directed by a man who is "the old man's Messiah," one Henry "Billy" Billson,

claimed to be ageless and magically powerful. The sect is said
to be comprised of about thirty-five young people, many of
them armed and dangerous....

I figure I better go down to the bus station with the tape and get the hell out of
town so I can sell the story to the press. And I mean right now.

I'm signing off. This recording is now—

*Hey there, bub. It's been a long time. You'd best turn that off. I wouldn't want to
burn up the machine when the lightning comes. And the lightning's come to you,
bub. Time to climb up, and ride the thunderbolt....*

El and Al vs. Himmler's Horrendous Horde From Hell

By

Mike Resnick

The Gestapo headquarters at Prinz-Albrecht-Strasse 8 looked like a cross between a foreboding Gothic castle and another foreboding Gothic castle. In a secret subterranean chamber *Reichsfuhrer* Heinrich Himmler thumbed through his grimmoires, searching for the proper spell. The United States had entered the war, the *Fuhrer* seemed not to understand the importance of that, and Himmler realized that it was up to him to secure the Third Reich's victory.

The *Fuhrer* was interested in the supernatural, gave it lip service, and encouraged his underlings to learn what they could about it—but he didn't really believe in it. At best, he admitted there *might* be something to it, and he funded research on it, but when push came to shove, he refused to trust in its power. And that left it to Himmler, who *did* believe, who *knew* it worked, to unlock the awesome force of the supernatural and harness its use for the Fatherland.

And he knew he was under the gun, because word had reached him that America's premier sorcerer had agreed to enter the fray against Germany. It galled him that the sorcerer was actually German by birth and now chose to battle against his homeland, but he knew how formidable the turncoat was.

Himmler thumbed through the texts, trying to find the single spell that would produce the results he required. When he thought he'd located it, he lit five black candles and placed them on the five points of a pentagram that he had drawn on the floor.

"Dark Messiah," he intoned, "I implore you to come to the aid of your most faithful servant. Give me the wherewithal to withstand this new enemy and its turncoat sorcerer, and I pledge that you shall be worshipped throughout the Third Reich for all eternity."

He then uttered three complex spells, spells that had never been combined before.

Finally, he reached into a cage that he kept next to the grimmoires, pulled out a newt, walked to the center of the pentagram, withdrew a knife, and slit the little amphibian's throat, placing the newt on the floor and watching its death throes.

When it expired, he uttered one more prayer, and concluded the obscene ritual with a cry of "*Shemhamforash!*"

And an ocean away, the Allies' greatest sorcerer climbed down the cellar stairs of his unimpressive frame house at 112 Mercer Street in Princeton, New Jersey. (Well, unimpressive but for the billboard in the empty lot next door, with an arrow pointing to his house and a huge photo of him accepting his Nobel Prize next to the statement in foot-high Tempo Bold letters that the World's Greatest Genius lived here.) As for the World's Greatest Genius himself, he never knew what the word *groupie* meant until the village of Princeton built the billboard. Now he had two sets of bodyguards, one to ward off Nazi and Japanese assassins, and the other to protect him from wildly passionate women. More than anyone else, he knew that his adopted country was up against not only the awesome might of Hitler's armies, but also the corrupt evil power that the *Fuhrer's* mightiest sorcerer, Heinrich Himmler, had at his command.

Albert Einstein was soon pouring over *his* holy books, preparing his spells to appeal to Tekno, a deity totally unknown to his German counterpart.

When he was ready, he closed the books, dipped his forefinger in the holy ink, and began chanting:

"The square of the hypotenuse equals the sum of the squares of the other two sides," he intoned. "Pi, carried to five decimal figures, is 3.14159. A circle has 360 degrees."

After another five minutes of chanting the spells, and a supplication to the Mathematical Trinity of Pythagoras, Euclid, and Fermat, he pulled a slide rule out of his pocket, held it over the books, and sacrificed it, breaking it and letting the two halves fall to the floor.

Then he uttered one last quadratic equation, and concluded the ritual with a triumphant cry of "*Q.E.D.!*"

"*Mein Gott*, you're *big!*" exclaimed Himmler as he looked at the army Satan had supplied.

There were thirteen of them, each blond and blue-eyed, each armed with a magical scimitar (which is kind of like a curved light-sabre, but effective rather than pretty), each ten feet tall, each wearing naught but a leather kilt.

"*Ow!*" cried the nearest as his head bumped against the ceiling, an action and a cry that was repeated twelve more times up and down the line.

"Duck your heads, *dumbkopfs!*" snapped Himmler.

"We bow to no one!" thundered one of them. "We'll raise the ceiling!"

So saying, he lifted his magical scimitar and punched a hole in the ceiling.

"You see?" he said with a smile. "There is nothing to it."

Well, he *tried* to say, "There is nothing to it," but somewhere between "There" and "is" a huge wooden desk fell through the hole and crashed onto his head. He collapsed beneath it, shoved it off to a side, and got groggily to his feet.

"Maybe I should have sacrificed *two* newts," muttered Himmler.

The other twelve golden-haired warriors decided to lower their heads.

"Excuse me, Boss …" began one of them.

"That's *Herr* Boss," Himmler corrected him.

"Excuse me, *Herr* Boss. But why have you summoned us from the very depths of hell?"

"Not that we mind it," added another quickly.

"Actually, it's much more pleasant here," said a third.

"A lot cooler as well," noted a fourth.

"You are here to defeat the American armed forces," said Himmler.

"What are they?" asked the first speaker, a contemptuous smile on his proud Aryan face. "Thirty or forty little men armed with rocks?"

"More like two million men, armed with the latest in aircraft, ships, cannons, automatic weapons, radar, and sonar."

"Against thirteen of us—and none of us even wearing any pants?" said one incredulously.

"You're Aryans!" bellowed Himmler. "Aryans triumph over everything!"

"Well, actually, my mother was half-Spanish," said one of them.

"And my Uncle Saul was Jewish."

"They always told me that George Washington Carver was a cousin."

"I will hear no more of this!" screamed Himmler. "You are Aryans, and you will follow my orders and march to victory, or I will return you to the fiery pits!"

"Where's Victory?" asked the last one in line. "I mean, if all we have to do is march there, I say we give it a try."

"Idiots!" said Himmler.

"Hey," said the last one, "*we're* not the ones who are sending thirteen men with skirts and pituitary conditions off to fight a mechanized army of two million."

"You are invulnerable!" insisted Himmler.

"Then how come my head hurt when the desk fell on it?" asked the first one.

"Wait a minute," said Himmler. He opened his grimmoire and thumbed through it. "Aha!" he said at last. "You are invulnerable to bullets, torpedoes, knives, swords, bombs, and certain social diseases that you're most likely to pick up in France, or perhaps North Hollywood, California. But I neglected to cast a spell to make you invulnerable either to stupidity or heavy objects falling on your heads. I will correct that oversight shortly."

"You'd better," sniffed the nearest one, rubbing the top of his head tenderly.

"I'll let you know the moment it's done," said Himmler. "What's your name?"

The huge supernatural Aryan looked blank. "I don't have one."

"Everyone has a name," insisted Himmler.

"Not me."

"Or me," said another.

"Me neither," said a third.

"You brought us here," said a fourth. "Probably you should be the one to name us."

"That seems reasonable," said Himmler. He walked up to the giant who was still rubbing his head. "You are Heinrich."

"Heinrich," repeated the Aryan. "Heinrich. Is there some reason for that?"

"It's my favorite name," answered Himmler. "It has a certain strength and nobility and just a touch of *je ne sais quoi* to it."

"How about me?" asked the next giant in line.

"I will call you Heinrich," said Himmler.

"But you're calling *him* Heinrich," protested the giant.

"You think there's only one Heinrich in the world?" demanded Himmler.

"There is enormous power and a certain gossamer gaiety to that name."

He went up and down the line, and when he was done he had a supernatural army composed of twelve Heinrichs and an Adolf (just in case he ever had to present one to the *Fuhrer*).

"Okay," said one of the Heinrichs. "We're here and we're named. Now what?"

"Now we wait to see what that scrawny little white-haired turncoat in America has planned for us, and then we meet his creatures in battle, cut out their hearts, tie them up with their own entrails, cut off their heads, spit down their necks, and—"

"*Stop!*" cried the nearest Heinrich, grabbing his stomach. "I'm going to be sick!"

Himmler sighed deeply. Maybe if he'd sacrificed an iguana....

"So what can your government do for you, Little Al?" said President Roosevelt, seated behind his desk in the Oval Office. "And make it snappy. I've got a war to fight."

"I am here to warn you of a dire threat to our troops," replied Einstein.

"What could be more dire than the German army?" said Roosevelt. "By the way, that's a hell of goiter on your hip. You'd better have it looked at."

"Hips don't have goiters," answered Einstein, pulling a crystal ball out of his pocket and sitting it down on the desk in front of the President. "Take a look."

Roosevelt leaned forward and stared. "There's nothing there."

"*The square root of one is one!*" intoned Einstein. "Now look at it."

"My God, that's remarkable!" exclaimed Roosevelt.

"I thought you should see it," said Einstein.

"How does she twirl them in both directions at the same time?"

Einstein bent over the desk. "Damn!" he said. "I forgot to adjust the channel. *Algebra kadabra!*"

"What's this?" asked Roosevelt, frowning and staring into the crystal. "It looks like a men's basketball team."

"It's thirteen invulnerable Aryan supermen, called up from the deepest pits of hell by none other than Heinrich Himmler," answered Einstein. "Defeating the German army will be a hard enough chore for General Eisenhower. *We* must destroy these super-Aryans before he has to face them."

"We?" said Roosevelt with a worried expression on his face. "You mean you and me?"

"No, sir," said Einstein. "We need you at the helm of State. What I've come for is Big El."

"Big El?"

"Your wife, Eleanor."

"She's yours, Little Al, and good luck to you," said Roosevelt with an uncon-
cerned shrug. "Now to business: what do you need to defeat Himmler's horrendous
horde from hell?"

"I just told you."

"You did?"

"Big El," repeated Einstein.

"Oh," said Roosevelt. "I thought you meant … never mind." He paused. "Are
you quite sure *she's* what you need?"

"Absolutely," said Einstein. "She's spent the last few years fighting big business,
and Southern bigots, and isolationists, and Republicans. She's in better fighting
shape than any other American."

"But can she stand up to these super Aryans?" persisted Roosevelt.

"If she and I together can't do it, with my mystical powers and her indomitable
spirit, then no one can."

"What the hell," said Roosevelt with a shrug. "If you feel she's what you need…."
He picked up the crystal ball and stared at it. "How do I bring back the original
image?"

"The girl with the … uh…?"

"Yes."

"*Kadabra algebra*," chanted Einstein. "Nothing to it." He walked to the door.
"I'll pick Eleanor up on my way out."

"Fine," said Roosevelt, staring at the crystal ball.

"We go now to save the world."

"Good," said Roosevelt without looking up. "Go."

Einstein opened the door. The last thing he heard before closing it behind him
was the President musing wistfully: "I wonder if she's got a phone number?"

"I'm not going to do it!"

Eleanor Roosevelt was standing in Einstein's book-lined basement, some
twenty feet away from him.

"But you're the only one who can, Big El," he said.

"Never!"

"I'll protect you," promised Einstein. "I've got a spell that even Fermat couldn't
solve. I'll invoke Isaac Newton himself."

"No!"

"But why not?" he asked, mystified. "You are potentially the greatest warrior woman who ever lived."

"I'm not wearing that skimpy little warrior princess outfit until I lose thirty-five pounds and get a dye job."

Einstein lowered his head and put his prodigious brain to work, finally looking up at her. "You've got it all wrong, Big El," he said soothingly. "You don't want to lose an ounce. If anything, you should *gain* some weight."

She looked at him as if he was crazy.

"Think about it," he urged her. "You're not trying to dazzle them with your beauty, but to terrify them with your muscle and your demeanor. The more formidable you look, the better."

"I'm a woman in her fifties," protested Eleanor. "I can't go around with a bare midriff and bare thighs and bare shoulders and…."

"We'll compromise," offered Einstein. "You can cover your left shoulder."

"And what is Himmler's horrendous horde wearing?" she asked.

"In my most recent visualization of the Cosmic All, they were wearing leather skirts and nothing else."

"Nothing else?" she repeated, arching an eyebrow.

"That's right."

"Skirts," she repeated. "Are they … you know?"

"They're ten-foot-tall killers," answered Einstein. "Does it make a difference what they do in their spare time?"

"I just want to know if they're sizing me up for the battle to come or ogling me."

Einstein stared at her thoughtfully for a long moment. "I don't think there's any doubt which they're doing," he said.

"All right," she said at last. "If my country needs me that badly, I'll do it. But along with the rest of the outfit, I have to have boots."

"You won't be traveling through rough terrain," he assured her. "We're just going to Gestapo headquarters."

"It's not that," said Eleanor. "I have varicose veins, and I want them covered up. Otherwise the battle's off."

He nodded his agreement. "Now let's talk about weapons."

"Right," she agreed. "I want a .44 Magnum, six hand grenades, and a repeating rifle."

"You'll have a sword."

"That's all?" she demanded.

"It will be an enchanted one." He pulled a kitchen knife out of his pocket, whispered "*Archimedes*" over it, and it instantly morphed into a wicked-looking sword, which he handed to her.

She looked at it briefly, and then said, "And these Aryans will all be armed with enchanted submachine guns, I presume?"

Einstein shrugged. "Who knows?"

"Well, I'd *like* to know," said Eleanor. "*You're* not going out there half-naked and armed with only a sword to face thirteen blond giants."

"I'll be there sharing the danger with you, Big El."

"Side by side?" she asked, relaxing visibly.

"Well, in the same city, anyway," he said. "While you're taking care of the horrendous horde, I'll be engaged in a duel of spells with Himmler himself."

"You're going to have a spelling bee while I'm fighting thirteen hate-filled barbarian Aryan giants?"

"Try not to understand me so fast," said Einstein. "If I don't subdue Himmler while you are occupying his fearless, merciless, invulnerable, incredibly strong warriors, he might conjure up fifty more."

Eleanor considered the situation. "I have a suggestion, Little Al," she said. "Why don't *I* handle Himmler while *you* take on his hideous horde?"

"That's his *horrendous* horde," Einstein corrected her.

"What's the difference?"

"One you have to fight single-handedly, and the other doesn't exist."

She merely glared at him.

Einstein fidgeted uncomfortably until she finally turned away from him. Then he spoke again: "You'd better get into your warrior princess outfit. In the interest of decorum (and possibly self-preservation) I'll turn my back while you change."

"How are we getting there?" she asked, starting to unbutton her suit coat, which she wore over her vest, which she wore over her blouse, which she wore over her slip, which she wore … but you get the idea.

"We're flying, all thanks to Leonardo," he said, staring at some complex formulae on his blackboard while she changed.

"Leonardo?" she repeated, staring at facsimiles of some of the Italian's notebooks on a shelf. "Have you actually found a way to turn us into winged creatures who can ride the warm thermals?"

"I beg your pardon?"

"Leonardo da Vinci's organic airplanes," she said.

"No," answered Einstein. "I'm talking about my friend Leonardo Schwartz. He has a private plane, and will be flying us there."

He continued staring at the blackboard for another five minutes.

"How's it coming, Big El?" he asked.

"I feel … what's the right word? … *flimsy*," she said uncomfortably. "You can turn around and look now, Little Al. But no whistling or catcalling—and especially no giggling," she added threateningly.

He turned and looked at the warrior princess. "I think I can resist the urge to whistle," he said earnestly.

"I wear more than this when I go to the beach," she complained. "*Much* more."

"It'll give you enormous freedom of movement when you take on the horrendous horde."

"How can you be sure there *is* a horrendous horde?" she said. "How do I know this wasn't all just a ruse so you could see me like this?"

"It came to me as I lay in bed last night," answered Einstein.

"A vision?"

"No, a ten-foot-high Aryan in a leather skirt," said Einstein. "I was hoping for a woman," he admitted. "Anyway, he suddenly appeared, said 'So *you're* what we have to destroy,' laughed his head off, and vanished."

"All right," said Eleanor heatedly. "It's time we taught the so-called Master Race a lesson."

"Fine. We'll drive to the private airport down the road and be on our way. I'll get the car."

She made him turn out all the lights and back up to the door so no neighbors or passersby could see her, and ten minutes later they were pulling up to Leonardo Schwartz's plane.

Einstein got out and opened the door for Eleanor. It took her a moment to work up her courage, but finally she stepped out of the car, enchanted sword in hand, and walked to the steps leading up to the plane.

"Who's your friend?" asked Schwartz. "My God, she's gorgeous!"

I didn't realize it was that dark a night, thought Eleanor.

"She is, isn't she?" agreed Einstein admiringly, holding out his hand to her. "Leo, say hello to Big El."

Schwartz took her hand and kissed it, then climbed into the cockpit.

"What are you staring at?" Eleanor demanded as Einstein kept smiling at her.

"More than your sword is enchanted," he said. "So is your outfit."

"My outfit?" she repeated, frowning.

"It was made for a gorgeous warrior princess, so that's what it's turned you into."

She looked down at herself, then smiled happily. "Thirty-five pounds, hell!" she exclaimed. "I've lost fifty if I've lost an ounce!"

She took the extra veil off her shoulder and handed it to him. "Here. I won't need *this* anymore."

Schwartz started the engines, while Einstein and Eleanor strapped themselves in.

"Thirteen of them, you say?" said Eleanor.

"That's right."

"Ten feet tall?"

"At least."

"Foul-tempered?"

"Worse. And spoiling for a fight."

The most beautiful warrior princess in America leaned back and smiled. "I can hardly wait," she said.

Himmler cooled his heels in Hitler's outer office for almost half an hour, and then was escorted inside.

"Ah, *Reichsfuhrer!*" said Hitler. "How good to see you again!"

"You just saw me three hours ago, *mein Fuhrer.*"

Hitler glared at him. "I do not like to be disagreed with," he said softly. "Except by Eva. *Mein Gott*, does that woman have a temper! You'd think anyone who could use a rolling pin like that would know how to cook!" The *Fuhrer* shuddered, then sat down. "So tell me about these supermen of yours."

"I told you this morning, *mein Fuhrer*," said Himmler.

"Do you know how many cities I've ordered destroyed since then?" snapped Hitler. "How many men I've had terminated? How many cigarettes I've smoked— and Turkish ones at that! Humor a busy man and tell me again!"

"There are thirteen of them," said Himmler. "Each stands more than ten feet tall, and each makes the vaunted Charles Atlas look like a ninety-eight-pound weakling."

"Charles Atlas?" repeated the *Fuhrer,* clearly impressed. "Isn't he the one who's in all those ads on the backs of, well … certain illustrated magazines, shall we say?"

"Comic books. Yes, sir," said Himmler. "Anyway, these thirteen perfect Aryan warriors are without peer."

"From what I hear they are also without clothes," said Hitler. "How can I send them to the Russian front?"

"I didn't summon them from the depths of hell to fight the Russians, *mein Fuhrer*," said Himmler. "They are here to ward off the attacks of the turncoat sorcerer Einstein."

"Don't mention that name to my face!" yelled Hitler.

"I apologize, *mein Fuhrer*," said Himmler quickly.

Hitler swiveled his chair until he was facing out a window, with his back to Himmler. "*Now* you can talk about him, *Reichsfuhrer.*"

"Yes, sir. Word has reached us from our spies in the White House that Einstein is about to unleash Mrs. Roosevelt upon us … and you know the success the President has had unleashing her on his other enemies."

"You were quite right to call them forth, *Reichsfuhrer,*" said Hitler. "Where will they meet her in battle?"

"We have no idea where she is at the moment," answered Himmler. "So I have concluded that the best course of action is to booby-trap Gestapo headquarters and wait for her there, since sooner or later she and Einstein"—Hitler whimpered at the mention of the name—"will come to Berlin and seek my Aryan supermen out."

"Maybe you should leave ten or twelve of them right here to protect *me*," suggested Hitler.

"They don't want you, sir."

"I beg your pardon!" screamed Hitler, spinning around in his chair to face Himmler.

"It's personal, sir," said Himmler.

"Explain!"

"I found an error in his Special Theory of Relativity and presented it in a speech to the Sorcerers' Society, right after their annual softball game."

"The greatest sorcerers in the world play softball?" asked Hitler, surprised.

"Well, usually the ball turns into a screeching Canadian goose on its way to the plate, and the bases grow legs and run off to Bismark, North Dakota, and—"

"I get the picture," interrupted the *Fuhrer*. "Continue."

"Anyway, I proved that D does not equal MC squared, and he has never forgiven me for that," said Himmler. "He and Mrs. Roosevelt are after *me*, sir, and they know they'll have to fight their way through my supermen to reach me."

"Have these superman all been trained in the use of the latest modern weapons?"

"They don't need them," answered Himmler. "They are masters of fisticuffs, wrestling, karate, kung fu, penjak, and the off-putting snide remark. Furthermore, they assure me they are invulnerable, that no bullet can pierce their proud Aryan skin."

"You don't say," said Hitler.

"I just *did* say, *mein Fuhrer.*"

"Maybe we should put it to the test. I haven't shot anyone since breakfast."

"I thought I saw them carrying the bullet-riddled body of the Postmaster General out of here while I was waiting to see you, sir," said Himmler.

"He was only five feet three inches tall," said Hitler with a shrug. "He hardly counts."

"All right, *mein Fuhrer*," said Himmler, clicking his heels together and snapping off a salute. "I'll bring them all to your office."

"Just a minute," said Hitler.

"Sir?"

"What are their names, so I will know how to address them?"

"There are twelve Heinrichs and an Adolf, sir."

"But no Einsteins?"

"No, sir."

"All right," said Hitler, opening his drawer and pulling out a tommygun. "Leave the Adolf behind. I certainly wouldn't want to hurt *him*."

"They are *all* invulnerable," Himmler assured him.

"We shall see."

"I'll have them here in ten minutes, *mein Fuhrer*."

"You're *sure* there are no Einsteins?"

"I'm sure."

"All right. Let's see if anything can pierce their proud Aryan skins."

And seven hundred and twenty-two bullets later he still didn't know what could pierce their skins, but he was damned sure he knew what *couldn't*.

The plane landed at a small airport about forty miles outside of London.

"This is as far as I go," announced Leonardo. "The Germans control everything between here and Berlin."

"Are you going to let a little thing like a few thousand anti-aircraft guns and fighter planes stop you when this scantily clad damsel is willing to face them armed with only a sword?" demanded Einstein.

"What the hell," said Leonardo. "When you put it that way...."

"Good!" said Einstein. "Refuel the plane and we'll be on our way. Big El and I will grab some dinner while you're standing out here in the pouring rain keeping a watchful eye on things."

He escorted Eleanor inside. They found a small snack shop, and soon were seated at a table.

"Everyone's staring," she noted.

"Probably seeing a half-naked warrior princess eating with a world-famous Nobel Prize winner isn't an everyday occurrence."

"So how are we going to get to Himmler's headquarters?" asked Eleanor.

"The direct approach is probably best," answered Einstein.

"The direct approach?"

He nodded. "When we get to downtown Berlin, I'll ask a cabbie."

"You think of everything, Little Al," she said admiringly. "How much trouble do we expect on the way in?"

"Well, I had hoped that Himmler was so anxious to have his horrendous horde meet you in personal combat that he would have ordered everyone to give us safe passage until we got there," said Einstein. "But if I'm wrong, then you may have to single-handedly conquer the German 4th, 6th, and 7th armored divisions—and that's if we make it over France without being shot down."

"Boy, those Nazis are *everywhere!*" said Eleanor grimly.

"Actually, I was thinking of the French," answered Einstein. "De Gaulle has never forgiven me for beating him at chess."

Eleanor studied the menu, then signaled the lone waitress.

"What'll it be, ma'am?" asked the girl.

"I'll have a hot fudge sundae, a piece of New York cheesecake, a chocolate éclair, and a slice of apple pie *a lá* mode, heavy on the whipped cream."

"Will you want anything to drink, ma'am? Tea, perhaps?"

"A chocolate malt."

Einstein ordered coffee, the waitress went off to the kitchen, and he stared curiously at Eleanor, who had a radiant smile on her face.

"I may keep this magical outfit forever, Little Al!" she enthused. "Twenty-three thousand calories, and I won't gain an ounce!"

"Not only that," said Einstein, "but you'll have all the energy you'll need for the battles that lay ahead of us. Well, of you."

"I feel sharp," she said. "Himmler's going to rue the day that he called these super Aryans up from hell."

"I'm starting to rue the day I called you up from hell!" growled Himmler as he faced his thirteen super Aryans.

"What did we do wrong *this* time?" asked Adolf.

"I don't mind that you can't march in formation. I don't mind that Heinrich Number 8 has a prostate problem and has to keep running to the john. I don't even mind that none of you has washed in all the time you've been here." He glared at them. "But I mind like all hell that nobody remembers to duck their heads or even use a door when they enter or leave a room. You're slowly but surely destroying the damned building. You!" he yelled, pointing at Heinrich Number 3. "Get that wistful smile off your face."

"But you mentioned home," protested Number 3.

"What the hell are you talking about?" demanded Himmler.

"There!" exclaimed Number 3. "You did it again!"

"Oh, shut up!" growled Himmler. "Just go down to the basement and try not to get into trouble. I'll call you when it's time to slaughter Mrs. Roosevelt."

"But it's dark and foreboding down there," whined Number 9. "And there are lurking shadows."

"So what?" said Himmler. "You guys are invulnerable."

"That doesn't make it less scary," said Number 5 petulantly.

"You can't be hurt," repeated Himmler. "That means nothing should scare you."

"Lots of things scare us," answered Adolf.

"Right," agreed Number 4. "Personally, I'm terrified of high cholesterol levels."

"And I'm afraid of tax auditors," added Number 7.

"Aggressive redheads named Thelma make me want to run for the hills," said Number 10. Suddenly he burst out crying.

"What's the matter with him?" asked Himmler.

"There *aren't* any hills in hell," explained Adolf.

"I've heard enough of this," exploded Himmler. "You are the ideals of German manhood, perfect in every way, at least from the neck down." Number 8 raised his hand to speak. "Except for Number 8's prostate," amended Himmler. "You are about to carry the hopes and dreams of the Third Reich into battle against the most formidable warrior and the most dangerous sorcerer that America has to offer. There can be no fears, no doubts, nothing but the absolute certainty that Aryans cannot ever lose."

"Uh … this warrior woman," said Number 1. "How big is she?"

"Not big enough!" roared Himmler. "You are the ideals of the Master Race. You are twice the size of normal men. You are invulnerable. You cannot feel pain, or fear, or fatigue. You represent everything that is fine and noble and worth keeping on this mongrel-filled planet. Now, let me hear it! Are you ready to triumph over the greatest warrior the Allies can provide?"

He wasn't sure, but he thought he counted seven yes's, five no's, and a maybe.

"There's Paris, coming up on your left," announced Leonardo as the plane banked to afford them a better view. "Last chance to stretch your legs and see the *Folies Bergère*."

"Why would I want to see the *Folies Bergère*?" asked Eleanor.

"I was thinking of Little Al," said Leonardo. "We used to have to drag him out of there almost every night during the last war."

"I found the atmosphere conducive to conjuring," said Einstein defensively.

"Usually he'd conjure up a spell and the prettiest girls would throw themselves at him."

"It was all for God and country," said Einstein. "Well, maybe excluding God. Besides, once I perfected it, it brought Mata Hari out of hiding and straight to me."

"With only one hundred and forty-three romantic pit stops along the way," said Leonardo.

"Maybe we should show you the Louvre," said Einstein, turning to Eleanor and changing the subject.

"Do they have any Norman Rockwells?" she asked.

Einstein shook his head. "Just da Vinci and Reubens and Michelangelo and that whole crowd."

"Foreigners all," she sniffed. She tapped Leonardo on the shoulder. "Just land. I'll kill a Nazi or two, make sure everything is in working order, and then we'll proceed to Berlin."

As they reached the outskirts of Paris, they began picking up anti-aircraft fire.

"That was a close one," said Leonardo as a shell exploded just to the left of the plane. "Hey, Little Al, are you sure you want to land here?"

"Don't interrupt!" said Einstein. His eyes were closed, and his hands were making mystical signs in the air. "*The acceleration of a body is directly proportional to the net unbalanced force and inversely proportional to the body's mass, a relationship is established between Force (F), Mass (m) and acceleration (a).*"

"What is he doing?" asked Leonardo.

"Magic!" whispered Eleanor in awestruck tones. "Don't interrupt him."

"*The squares of the periods of revolution of the planets about the Sun are proportional to the cubes of their mean distances from it,*" chanted Einstein. Suddenly he relaxed and looked at his companions. "Okay," he said. "The plane will be invulnerable to German fire for the next seventy-three minutes. Now you can land."

"By God!" said Leonardo. "How can the Germans stand up to a brain like that?"

"It's not that simple," said Einstein. "My magic only works on normal Nazis, not on Himmler's super Aryans. For that, we need some very *special* magic, some spell that's never been cast before."

"So cast it," said Leonardo.

"I'm working on it," said Einstein. He closed his eyes, held out his hands, and chanted, "*E equals MC cubed!*"

"The engine just died," announced Leonardo.

"Damn!" said Einstein as they glided silently toward the ground. "I thought I had it this time!"

"All right," said Himmler. "The *Fuhrer* is coming by to inspect you any minute now. I want you to line up alphabetically."

"But there are twelve Heinrichs," said Heinrich Number 9.

"All right," said Himmler. "By height."

"We're all the same size."

"Draw straws," snarled Himmler.

"Give us some pencils," said Heinrich Number 6. "And where do you want us to draw them?"

Heinrich Number 8 emerged from the bathroom and rejoined the others. "Did I miss anything important?" he asked.

"Shut up!" snapped Himmler. "I want you all to line up numerically."

"Right to left, or left to right?" asked Heinrich Number 1.

"Yes!" yelled Himmler.

After a few moments of confusion, the twelve super Aryan Heinrichs were finally in line.

"Where do *I* go?" asked Adolf.

"Alphabetically," said Himmler.

"But they're all numerical."

"All right—numerically."

"But I don't have a number."

"Adolf, you are an idiot!" screamed Himmler.

"*What did you call me?*" bellowed a familiar voice from behind him.

"Oh, shit!" said Himmler as his knees began to tremble.

"150 propositions from French men before we even leave the airport!" said Eleanor wearily. "Can the super Aryans be any more exhausting?" She paused, frowning. "Maybe having this figure isn't all that it's cracked up to be. I never got this tired fighting off Republicans."

"I think your response—the one that scared them all away—was a stroke of genius," replied Einstein. "Three little words and they were dispersed to the four winds."

"I'll have to remember them the next time we're in France," said Eleanor. "*Marry me first*," she intoned. "Suddenly they looked like a bunch of sprinters trying out for the Olympics."

"Brilliant," agreed Einstein. "I wouldn't try it in Beirut, though, or even Dubai."

"I wonder where all the Nazis are," said Eleanor. "We didn't see a single one."

"Probably at the *Folies Bergère* or maybe the Lido," answered Einstein. "Or robbing art treasures from the Louvre. They do that a lot. I suppose we could pop over there and stop them?"

"Why bother?" she asked. "You already said there are no Norman Rockwells there. There are probably no Virgil Finlays or Frank R. Pauls either. Just a bunch of guys with funny names. No, Little Al, I've stretched my gorgeous cellulite-free legs now. Let's move on to Berlin."

"There's the plane," he said, as they entered the small, private airport where Leonardo had set it down and was trying to start the engine.

Suddenly they found their way blocked by five armed Nazis in uniform.

"I've been wondering where you guys were," said Eleanor, sword in hand. "Prepare to meet your maker."

"Meet my baker?" said one with a hearing aid. "What on earth is she talking about?"

"Your maker, your maker!" she snapped.

"I'm still confused," said the Nazi. "Is she talking about one of my parents?"

"I'm talking about your God!" roared Eleanor.

"You'll have to talk to someone else, then," he replied. "We members of the Master Race aren't allowed to believe in God."

"That's not entirely true," said one of his companions. "We're allowed to worship Mars, God of War."

"And I think we can worship Colgate, God of Healthy Teeth," said another.

"Enough!" snapped Eleanor. "Prepare to die!"

"If I'm going to prepare for it," said another Nazi, "I have to go back to Hamburg and write my will, and pay off all my creditors, and tell my wife where I really was during that snowstorm last February. I don't suppose you could wait right here for eight weeks until I take care of all that and come back, could you?"

"You are the talkiest soulless sadistic fiends I've ever met!" said Eleanor. "Well, since Alf Landon and Wendell Willkie, anyway. Now, are you going to fight or are you going to talk?"

"You *are* Big El, aren't you?" asked still another Nazi.

"That's right."

"Then I guess we're going to talk. We have orders to escort you to Berlin, and not to rob Herr Himmler's Horrendous Horde From Hell of the fun of slowly dismembering you."

Eleanor turned to Einstein. "What do you think, Little Al?"

He turned to Leonardo's plane. "*F equals MC squared!*" he chanted.

Both wings fell off, and one of the tires went flat.

Einstein turned back to the Nazis. "You have transportation?"

"Of course."

"Then I guess we're going with you," said Einstein.

As they were climbing aboard the Nazis' plane, one of them pulled Eleanor aside.

"I don't mean to be forward," he said, lowering his voice so only she could hear it. "But if, on the thousand-to-one chance that you survive your forthcoming duel to the death with Himmler's Horrendous Horde, would you like to get together afterward? I'd love to show you the sights of Berlin at night."

She gave him a smile. "Marry me first," she whispered.

He sat as far from her as possible, and didn't speak to her for the duration of the flight or the rest of this story.

The red phone on the President's desk began ringing, and Roosevelt picked it up.

"You know who this is?" said a voice with a heavy German accent.

"I can guess," said Roosevelt. "What do you want?"

"You know your wife is on her way here with that little turncoat Ein ... Ein ... "—he forced the word out—"Einstein."

"I'm aware of it."

"You really think to destroy my super Aryans?" demanded Hitler.

"You have nothing to fear but Eleanor herself," said Roosevelt.

"I have a proposition," said Hitler. "Why don't we let the coming battle between your wife and my Aryans determine the war—winner take all?"

"Why should I make a deal like that when half your army is freezing to death in Russia?"

"You're not supposed to know that!" screamed Hitler. There was an uneasy pause. "I mean—"

"Forget it," said Roosevelt. "Now, if you want to make a little side bet ..."

"A million marks to a million dollars!" said Hitler promptly.

"Come on, Adolf," said Roosevelt. "You've devalued your currency so much that a million marks barely buys a loaf of bread."

"But it is good German bread!" protested the *Fuhrer*.

"Not a chance."

"Wait a minute!" said Hitler. "We own France, too! A million dollars against a million francs!"

"Goodbye, Adolf."

Roosevelt hung up the phone and went back to studying his crystal ball.

"Welcome to Berlin, *Fraulein*," said one of the guards at the airfield.

"Thank you," said Eleanor, who saw no reason to tell him, or anyone else, that she was actually a *Frau*.

"You may find our nights a little chilly for your apparel."

"Have you a nice, heavy, shapeless coat that I can use to cover myself?" she asked.

"*NO!*" cried all the other guards.

The guard shrugged helplessly. "I guess not."

"I'm sure I'll be fine," she said.

"You are escorting her to Gestapo headquarters," said one of the Nazis who had accompanied her from Paris.

"Just her?"

Einstein stepped forward. "Me too."

"You too?" repeated the guard. "That's funny. You don't look too-ish."

"Actually," said another guard, "he does."

"Just get us there," said Einstein. "We're wasting time."

"Who are you to give us orders?"

"I'm Little Al, that's who," he said. Suddenly he closed his eyes and began chanting a spell. "*The area of a triangle is one half times the base length times the height of the triangle.*"

"Yes, sir," said the guard as he and his companions seemed to fall into a trance-like state. "This way, sir. Watch your step, sir."

"Thank you," said Einstein.

The guards led them to a truck.

"That looks uncomfortable," said Eleanor. "Haven't you got a car?"

"The *Fuhrer* has outlawed all makes and models but the Volkswagen," came the answer. "Except for his own fleet of Cadillacs, that is."

"So?"

"The Volkswagen is the smallest, most uncomfortable car in all of Europe," said the guard. "It reminds me of a beetle the way it hugs the ground. I know the *Fuhrer* is perfect and infallible and all that, but if he really thinks these undersized monstrosities are ever going to be popular...."

"They don't use much gas, though," noted one of his companions.

"You say that as if the world will ever run out of gas," said the guard.

"Science fiction writers are predicting that it may someday be so rare that it will cost as much as ten U.S. cents a gallon."

The guard shrugged his shoulders. "What can you expect from a bunch of unemployable daydreamers?" he said contemptuously. He turned to Eleanor and Einstein. "Are you ready?"

"Yes," said Eleanor.

"Then climb into the back and we'll be on our way."

"I may need a little help," said Einstein.

Three of the guards boosted him into the truck, then looked their disappointment when Eleanor was able to climb in on her own.

As they rode, avoiding debris and craters in the street, they could hear the whistling sounds of bombs falling, followed by deafening explosions as they tore into the heart of Berlin. Eleanor looked out the back of the truck and saw several buildings on fire after a direct hit.

"It would appear that the Luftwaffe is no match for our American and British bombers," she remarked.

"Oh, *that*," said a guard with no show of emotion. "The *Fuhrer* assures us that we can shoot down the Allies' planes whenever we want."

"If you can, why don't you?" asked Eleanor. "The whole city is ablaze."

"The *Fuhrer* has explained that he only lets the bombers through to save money on electricity. You have no idea how expensive it is to light a modern city at night, *Fraulein*."

Eleanor and Einstein exchanged knowing looks.

"I just saw the two of you exchanging knowing looks," said a guard. "What do they mean?"

"They mean we agree that you've found a cost-effective way to light your city," said Einstein.

"It also saves us the cost of maintaining our streets," said the guard. "You know—painting lines down the middle, filling in potholes, that sort of thing."

"It does?" said Einstein curiously.

The guard smiled and pointed to a series of recently made craters. "No more streets. Now that money can be directed to other enterprises."

Einstein turned to Eleanor. "I'm surprised the war is still going on," he remarked.

"As soon as we find an economical way to cure eight hundred thousand cases of frostbite on the Russian front, we should finally have this war under control," said the guard.

"So you see, you're wasting your time," added another guard. "The war is all but over. Why chance having a gorgeous creature like your companion get torn to shreds by thirteen giant super Aryans?"

"Right," chimed in a third. "My apartment is just in the next block. We could stop there right now. You could sit in a corner and bury your nose in a book, while we and the little lady are having a party."

"What did you call me?" demanded Eleanor.

"The little lady," repeated the guard.

A tear rolled down her cheek. "That's the nicest thing anyone has said to me in thirty years."

"So how about the party?" persisted the guard. "Are we all agreed?"

Eleanor uttered her semi-magical three words, and suddenly the truck picked up speed and headed straight for Gestapo headquarters.

Himmler entered the huge subterranean chamber, clapped his hands together, and called for his super Aryans' attention.

"They're on their way," he announced. "They'll be here any minute. I want you looking your best and most formidable. Line up."

"How?" asked Adolf.

"In a straight line, of course."

"I mean, by what criterion?"

"Numerically."

Heinrichs 1 through 12 lined up in numerical order.

"Where do *I* go?" asked Adolf.

"Just stand at one end or the other," said Himmler wearily.

"Which end?"

"*I don't care!*" yelled Himmler.

Heinrich Number 8 raised his hand. "Excuse me a minute," he said, walking toward the bathroom with increasing haste. "I'll be right back."

"Take *his* place," said Himmler.

"But my name doesn't begin with an H."

"Just do it!" screamed Himmler.

Adolf shrugged, walked over, and stood between Heinrichs 7 and 9. "But I am in this spot under false pretenses," he complained.

"I could have been a farmer," muttered Himmler. "I was really good at milking cows and harvesting corn. I was happy sitting atop a tractor. The sheep and pigs never talked back to me. Mostly, I didn't have to deal with a bunch of empty-headed super-beings."

Heinrich Number 8 returned from the bathroom and approached his fellow Aryans.

"He's in my place," he whined, pointing to Adolf.

"Move to the end of the line," Himmler told Adolf.

"Which end?"

Himmler pulled his revolver out of his holster and fired six quick shots at

Adolf's chest. They all bounced off.

"I'm invulnerable," Adolf pointed out. "Shooting can't hurt me."

"But it makes *me* feel better," replied Himmler, holstering his gun. "Now go the end of the line. And before you ask, the left end."

"My left or your left?"

Himmler hurled his revolver at Adolf's head. It bounced off and fell to the floor.

"I'll get it for you," offered Heinrich Number 3.

"Don't bother," said Himmler disgustedly, walking over to pick it up. "You'll forget where you were standing."

"On my feet," said Heinrich Number 3.

"Why did I ever think Aryans were the Master Race?" muttered Himmler.

Suddenly a red light began flashing.

"They're here!" said Himmler excitedly. "They should be entering this chamber in less than three minutes. *Achtung!*"

The thirteen super Aryans stood at attention.

"The forthcoming slaughter is what you were created for," said Himmler, walking up and down in front of them. "I want you to show Big El absolutely no mercy."

"Even if she begs?" asked Heinrich Number 11.

"She won't," Himmler assured them. "She's made of sterner stuff. It's your job to dismantle her and spread that sterner stuff all over the room."

Heinrich Number 10, the one with the queasy stomach, put his hand to his mouth, then raced off to the bathroom.

"He's just sensitive," said Adolf apologetically.

"What about Little Al?" asked Heinrich Number 2.

"You leave Little Al to me," said Himmler. "You guys just concentrate on Big El."

"Not to worry, sir," said Heinrich Number 4. "I'll cut her heart out and eat it. I'll decapitate her, gouge out her eyes, and use her head as a bowling ball. I'll—"

Heinrich Number 10, who was just emerging from the bathroom, listened, groaned, and ran right back in, while Himmler found himself wondering how Geronimo or Shaka Zulu would have handled these problems.

"You're not nervous, are you?" asked Einstein as the guards escorted them down the dark winding stairs to the Aryans' chamber.

"Not in the least," answered the closest guard. "It's not as if *I* have to fight you."

"I was talking to Big El," said Einstein.

"Is my make-up smudged?" asked Eleanor.

"No."

"And my hair's not messed up?"

"Not a bit."

"Then I'm not nervous," she answered. "How about you, Little Al? After all, you're going to be facing the notorious Heinrich Himmler while all I'm doing is fending off thirteen foul-tempered and invulnerable giants."

"I feel sharp," said Einstein. "And I'm getting close to the Ultimate Spell. Once I've got it, he'll never know what hit him."

"The Ultimate Spell?" asked Eleanor.

"Watch this," said Einstein. He raised his arms, closed his eyes, and chanted "*E equals NC squared.*"

Suddenly all the guards' pants vanished.

"Damn!" muttered Einstein. "I'm so close! I can feel it!"

"Can we have our pants back?" said one of the guards. "Herr Himmler is a stickler for decorum."

Einstein shrugged. "I don't know where they are."

"We ought to get *something* out of this," said another guard. "Say it again and make *her* clothes vanish."

"Just be grateful I didn't make *you* vanish," said Einstein.

"You can do that?" said a third guard. "You'd be a handy guy to have around in case we get transferred to the Russian front."

They came to a massive steel door. The lead guard opened it, and a moment later they were facing Himmler and his thirteen super Aryans.

"Finally!" said Himmler. "You have no idea how long I have waited for this moment!" He looked at the guards. "You're not wearing any pants."

"Neither are your supermen," said a guard defensively.

"This is wartime. There are the usual shortages. We don't have enough material to make pants for them. But you already *had* pants."

"Look," said Einstein. "If you guys want to argue, we can go out for coffee."

"This is Berlin!" snapped Himmler. "You would go out for beer! However," he added with an evil grin, "you are not going anywhere. Here you have come, and here you shall die."

"That's wrong," said Heinrich Number 5. "It should be: 'Here you have come, and here you shall stay.' There's a certain poetic unity to it that way."

"I don't know," said Heinrich Number 7. "I think the problem was that he said '*shall* die' instead of '*will* die.' Somehow 'will die' sounds more definite, if you know what I mean."

Soon nine of the Heinrichs were arguing the finer points of language, and Himmler turned to Eleanor and Einstein. "What will you pay me for thirteen

giants with a collective IQ of 73?" Finally he turned back to the super Aryans.
"*Shut up!*" he screamed.

They fell silent instantly.

"All right," he said. "Are we ready to begin?"

Heinrich Number 9 held up his hand.

"What now?" demanded Himmler.

"How do you want us to fight her? All at once, or one at a time?"

"I hadn't really considered it," admitted Himmler.

"I have a suggestion," said Einstein.

"Yes?"

"All they're good for is fighting, right? So have a competition: let them fight
each other for the right to face Big El."

Himmler frowned. "I have a feeling there's something exceptionally silly about
that idea, but I can't quite put my finger on it."

Suddenly Adolf stepped forward. "*I* will fight her," he announced.

"Why you?" demanded Heinrich Number 1.

"Because I am unique. I am named for the *Fuhrer*, whereas you twelve are named
for this insignificant little wimp here, meaning no offense, Herr Himmler."

"Okay," agreed Heinrich Number 1. "When you're right, you're right."

"But you can lend a hand if things get hairy," added Adolf.

"Are you calling me hairy?" demanded Eleanor furiously. "Let's start right now!"

"Wait!" cried Einstein.

Everyone turned to him.

"What is it?" asked Eleanor.

"We can't have them all piling on you if things start going well for our side,"
said Einstein.

"And I don't want you to be able to come after me if you actually survive and
your blood's up," added Himmler. He turned to Einstein. "How shall we separate
them?"

"The same way they separate the lions and tigers from the audience at a circus,
I suppose," replied Einstein.

"I agree," said Himmler. "You two"—he signaled to Adolf and Eleanor—"stand
over there."

When they had moved where he wanted them, he turned back to Einstein.
"Spell Number 1209?" he suggested.

Einstein considered it. "Make it 1209-A. We won't need all the stools for the
lions to perch on."

They chanted the spell together, and within seconds Eleanor and Adolf found themselves in the middle of a steel cage some thirty feet in diameter.

"Shall the match begin?" suggested Himmler.

"A steel cage match," mused Einstein. "I intuit an incredibly profitable commercial enterprise here once the war's over."

"May I proceed to tear her into small pieces now?" asked Adolf.

"Just you try it," snarled Eleanor. "This is Big El you're facing!" She drew her sword and faced him.

"Say your prayers, female!" bellowed Adolf, reaching out to grab her. She slapped his huge hand with the flat of her enchanted blade.

"Ow!" he yelled. "That hurt!"

"Not as much as it's going to hurt when I cut your foul heart out," she said, advancing toward him menacingly.

"Wait a minute!" yelled Adolf, backing away. "Fins! Fingers! Time out!"

"What is it?" demanded Eleanor.

Adolf turned to face Himmler. "You told us we were invulnerable!" he said accusingly. "I've never felt pain before, but from everything I've heard and read about it, *that* was pain!"

"Don't be such a crybaby!" snapped Himmler. "You are fighting for the honor of the Aryan race!"

"Make her get rid of the sword!" whined Adolf. "Then I'll fight her."

Himmler walked over to where Eleanor stood and pressed his face against the steel cage. "I don't suppose you'd consider relinquishing your weapon in the name of sportsmanship?" he said. "I mean, *he* doesn't have one. That would make it a fair fight."

"A fair fight?" she repeated. "He's ten feel tall and all muscle!"

"All right," said Himmler with a shrug. "We'll just have to let it be known that the only way the Americans are willing to fight is when they have an unfair advantage."

Eleanor stared at her sword, then carefully leaned it up against the bars.

"Prepare to die, female!" cried Adolf, launching himself at her.

A moment later he was flying across the ring, where he crashed into the bars and fell heavily to the floor.

"What the hell happened?" demanded Himmler.

Adolf frowned. "I bounced off her."

A triumphant smile appeared on Eleanor's face. "I forgot to tell you," she said. "I'm armored in my righteousness."

"Be subtle," urged Himmler. "Use vectors and angles and misdirection."

Adolf checked the pockets of his kilt. "I don't have any of those things."

"Then just use your superior Aryan strength and ruthlessness!" growled Himmler.

"At the same time?" asked Adolf.

"Just do it!" screamed Himmler.

Adolf began approaching Eleanor very carefully. This time, instead of blindly charging her, he reached a hand out to grab her.

"Ow!" he yelled, rubbing his jaw where she slapped him. "What did you do *that* for?"

"Don't touch me there!" said Eleanor.

He approached her again, reached out again, and got slapped for his trouble again.

"Don't touch me *there*, either!" said Eleanor severely.

Adolf made a T for "time out" with his hands, and walked to a neutral corner. "I've got to think this out," he said.

"There's nothing to think!" yelled Himmler. "You're huge, she's not. You're muscle-bound, she's not. You're a man, she's not. You're an Aryan, she's not."

"Right," said Adolf. "And I'm smart, and she's not."

"Well, you're an Aryan, anyway," said Himmler.

"I need a strategy," said Adolf. "She won't let me touch her in any of the usual places."

"What do you mean—'the usual places'?" said Himmler. "This is a battle to the death, not a Saturday night date!"

"What do you suggest?" asked Adolf.

"Snap her spine like a toothpick!" screamed Himmler. "Crush her skull like a walnut!"

"Oh my God!" moaned Heinrich Number 10, clutching his stomach. "I'm gonna be sick again!"

"All right," said Adolf, working himself into a killing rage and facing Eleanor. "Now you're gonna get it!"

When he was almost within arm's reach of her, she looked down at his kilt and giggled.

"What's so funny?" he growled.

"Your fly is unzipped."

He looked down and she landed a powerful karate kick to his chin.

"I don't *have* a fly!" he groaned as he careened across the ring.

"You know," said Eleanor to Einstein, "I think there's a distinct possibility that I didn't need the sword *or* the outfit."

"That wasn't fair!" said Adolf petulantly as he got back on his feet.

"All's fair in love and war," said Eleanor.

"Love?" he repeated, puzzled. "What's love got to do with it?"

"This is all a joke, isn't it, *Herr* Himmler?" said Eleanor. "You've got the *real* super Aryans hidden somewhere else in the building."

"*Kill her, godammit!*" screeched Himmler.

Suddenly Adolf's gaze fell on the magical sword that rested against the side of the cage. He stared at it for a few seconds, then took a tentative step in its direction.

"Don't touch it!" said Eleanor in severe tones.

"Why not?" he asked.

"It's not yours," she said.

"Oh," replied Adolf, momentarily chastened. Then: "So what?"

"That would be cheating," said Eleanor.

"Pick the damned thing up and cut her head off!" yelled Himmler.

"It's not mine," explained Adolf. "That would be cheating."

"I absolve you. Now kill her!"

"I warn you," said Eleanor. "Don't touch it."

"You can't scare me," said Adolf. "I've been absolved."

"Do you even know what that means?" she asked.

"Sort of," he said. "It's kind of like being forgiven for staying up all night reading your father's dirty magazines."

"So you're really going to pick it up?"

"Yes."

"Even though it's immoral to steal someone else's sword?" she persisted.

He turned to Himmler. "What about that?" he asked.

"It's your moral imperative to kill her!" ordered Himmler.

"Well," said Eleanor, "you were warned."

Adolf reached out and grabbed the sword. Instantly the room was filled with a crackling, buzzing sound—an effect that really bad 1950s science fiction movies would combine with static electricity a decade later, only this was both real and deadly—and he briefly glowed a brilliant yellow, then mauve, and then vanished.

Eleanor walked over, picked up her magic sword, and faced the twelve Heinrichs.

"Who's next?" she asked sweetly.

"You!" said Himmler, pointing to Heinrich Number 1. "Remember that you're fighting for the supremacy of Germany and the Aryan race. Now get in there and kill her."

"Couldn't we just cut cards instead?" asked Number 1.

"We don't have any cards," said Himmler.

"Hopscotch!" said Number 1. "We could play hopscotch!"

"Bah!" spat Himmler. "You're useless." He looked at the others. "You!" He pointed to Heinrich Number 6. "Kill her."

"Come on!" said Eleanor, twirling her magic sword as if it were a baton. "I'm ready for you!"

"There's nothing I'd like more than to kill her, Herr Himmler," said Number 6. "But my lumbago's been acting up, and—"

"You're physically perfect!" screamed Himmler. "You can't have lumbago!"

"Sure I can," he said, rubbing his shoulder. "It's really bothering me!"

"That's your shoulder, idiot! Lumbago affects your lower back."

"I was just scratching an itch," said Number 6 defensively. He moved his hand to his lower back. "That lumbago's really bothering me." He turned to Eleanor. "I'm sorry, Big El. There's nothing I'd like more than to kill you, but you can see that it wouldn't be a fair fight."

"I'll even the odds," she said.

"How?"

"I'll fight with one eye closed."

Number 6 suddenly groaned and clutched at his chest. "I think I'm coming down with pellagra, too!"

"You get pellagra from an inadequate diet," yelled Himmler. "And super Aryans don't eat!"

"You can't make me fight her on an empty stomach!" protested Number 6.

Himmler turned to Einstein. "This just isn't working out," he said apologetically. "All right. I want all twelve Heinrichs in the cage with her!"

"Little Al?" said Eleanor. "I could use some help."

Einstein faced the twelve super Aryans, closed his eyes, reached his arms out, and chanted, "*E equals MC squared!*"

And suddenly all twelve Aryans were gone, replaced by twelve little mushroom clouds.

"Son of a bitch!" exclaimed Einstein. "I finally got it right!"

"You haven't heard the last of me!" promised Himmler. He closed his eyes, reached his arms out, and chanted, "*I was only following orders!*" There was a puff of smoke, and suddenly Eleanor and Einstein were alone in the vast chamber.

"Well, it looks like we scored another victory for Truth, Justice, and the American Way, Big El," said Einstein.

"Your spell actually worked, Little Al," she said. "I'm so proud of you!" Suddenly she frowned. "How are we going to get home?"

"Not to worry," said Einstein. "I've got it covered."

And moments later they were in the White House, having traveled there exactly the way the brighter readers of this story anticipated. As they parted outside the Oval Office, she returned the enchanted sword to him.

"Can I keep the outfit?" she asked. "Just for special occasions?"

"Sure, Big El," said Einstein. "You've earned it."

Then she went off to her room, and Einstein entered the office.

"We're back, Mr. President!" he announced triumphantly.

Roosevelt reluctantly looked up from the crystal ball he'd been studying intently.

"Oh," he said. "Were you gone?"

From Hell's Heart

By

Nancy A. Collins

I am hesitant to relate the tale I am about to tell, largely because it does nothing
to bolster my claims of sanity. But if I am to convince others of my innocence
in this matter, I have no choice but to recount the singular events that have
lead me to this cold cell.

I am first-generation Canadian, my parents having migrated from their native
Scotland to this wild and boundless land. I have long harbored a deep fascination
with the rough-and-tumble lifestyle of the French-Canadian *couriers de bois*, those
rugged pioneers who helped shape our fledgling nation. Because of this, I left my
home in Toronto for the wilds of what, until recently, was known as Rupert's Land,
with the intention of becoming a trapper. However, my enthusiasm proved far
greater than my woodscraft, and I found it all I could do to survive the first heavy
snowfall.

As luck would have it, while on a visit to a trading post, I made the acquaintance
of a certain Dick Buchan and Ben Martin. They, too, were new to the trapping

game and having a hard time of it. We agreed that it was a lonesome and difficult business, especially during the long winter months, and decided to pool our resources and become partners, running our traplines from a home shanty near the vast shores of God's Lake.

Of the three who comprised our rustic enterprise, I was the youngest. Buchan was, at the ripe old age of twenty-seven, the eldest of our group. He was a tall, well-developed specimen with copper-red hair and a beard to match, and claimed to have a wife and child in Winnipeg. Martin was a year or so his junior, and as stout and strong as an oak barrel, with dark brown hair and a feisty sense of humor.

Come the thaw, my partners and I transported our bundles of fur to the trading post at God's Lake. From there they were loaded onto boats and ferried the two hundred miles to the York Factory on the southwestern shore of Hudson Bay.

After dividing our profits three ways, we discovered we had done far better together than we ever could have alone. We had done so well, in fact, we were able to hire on a Cree Indian, who went by the name of Jack, to cook for us and keep an eye on the home shanty while we were off tending our traplines.

As far as I could tell, Jack was older than any of us, and claimed to be the son of an *ogimaa*, which is a cross between a chief and a shaman, to hear him tell it. I don't know about any of that, but I do know he could play a mean fiddle, which he often did to pass the time on those long winter nights.

I am not going to lie and say that we went without arguments or differences of opinion. But for the most part, despite being brought together by happenstance and necessity, the four of us found one another's company agreeable. This I attribute to the fact three of us shared similar backgrounds and had each, as a boy, worshipped the hardy voyageurs and colorful Mountain Men who loomed so large in our newborn nation's identity, while Jack knew little English, although he did speak French passing well.

Summer is short in this part of the world, full of mosquitoes and dragonflies, and Fall is shorter still. The first snows came early, turning the towering pines and hemlocks white by the third week of October. The next day Jack frowned at the sky and muttered something about not liking something on the wind, but I did not pay him much heed. Although we cursed the cold and having to trudge about on snow shoes, we knew this meant the beaver, fox, and rabbit would be changing into their prized winter coats all the sooner.

Our humble home shanty was the hub for traplines that extended for twenty miles each in various directions, like spokes on a wheel. Some followed the borders of the lake and the streams that fed into it, and caught mostly beaver, otter, muskrat, and mink. Others extended inland, and brought us raccoons, foxes, lynx, coyote, and the occasional bear. Along these routes were a series of tilts—squat ten-by-six structures with sharply angled roofs, fashioned from notched spruce logs trimmed by hand to fit tightly together without a single iron nail—that served both as supply depots and shelter. During the trapping season, I and my companions would set out along one of these "spokes," checking and resetting our traps along the way, until we reached the end of our territory, then we would head back via an adjacent line.

The snow was already six inches deep, even more where the wind had driven it into drifts, when we set out to check the lines. Martin headed west, while Buchan and I headed northeast, leaving Jack to tend the fires at the home shanty. Each of us was outfitted with an Indian sledge, which we towed behind us, and enough provisions to withstand a fortnight in the bush. The sled dogs were to remain with Jack, to be held in reserve for swift traveling and transporting heavy loads to and from the trading post.

As I said, Buchan and I set out together. The plan was for me to follow him to the first tilt on the line, then he and I would go our separate ways. I would head north in the direction of Red Cross Lake, while he would head east, toward Edmund Lake.

We set out just after dawn and arrived at our destination just after noon. We spent the remaining hours of daylight left to us weatherproofing our shelter by gathering moss and alder twigs, which we used to line the walls and roof, while throwing out the rotted remains of the previous season's insulation.

As the sun set, we crawled through the two-foot square opening at the tilt's gable end, tacking off the entrance with a piece of elk hide. In the far corner of the shelter was a portable stove fashioned from a long, rectangular hard-tack tin affixed to a short pipe that vented through the roof. We lost no time in putting the makeshift fireplace to good use, and soon the interior was quite warm. It was a snug fit for two grown men, but comfortable enough. As I bedded down for the night, I could hear the wind whistling mournfully about the eaves of the shelter. Every now and again the gusts would rattle the hide that served as our door, as if something outside was desperately trying to find its way in. However, I was too tired to entertain such fancies for long, and soon fell asleep.

At some point later that night I was shaken from a sound slumber to find Buchan's urgent voice in my ear. I opened my eyes to darkness so black I could not see my companion's face, though I knew from the heat of his breath that it had to be inches from my own. Although I had no way of knowing what time it was, I instinctively knew it was midnight.

"What's the matter?" I mumbled.

"Do you hear that?" Buchan whispered.

I focused my senses, still blurred by sleep, but all I heard was the howling of the wind.

"There's nothing out there," I replied tersely. "Go back to sleep."

"Are you sure?" Buchan asked, his unseen fingers digging into my shoulder.

I listened again, and this time I became aware of a weird noise off in the distance: half-roar, half-wail. "It's probably something in one of the traps," I said. "A wolf, perhaps, or maybe a lynx. They can make a hellacious racket when they're caught."

"You're probably right," he said, apparently mollified by my explanation. With that, Buchan rolled over and went back to sleep.

I lay there for a long moment, listening to the cry laced within the wind, trying to identify it, but the noise soon fell silent. I told myself that whatever was responsible for making it had died or moved on, and returned to my slumber. However, the dreams that filled the remainder of my night were fitful, providing little in the way of rest.

The next day I rose with the sun, only to find my companion already up and about. As I relieved myself against a nearby tree, I spotted Buchan kneeling in the snow roughly fifty yards from the tilt, checking one of his traps. Without warning he suddenly cut loose with a string of particularly virulent curses.

"What's the matter?" I called out.

"You were right about that noise last night," he shouted back. "There's something in the trap!"

"What did you catch?" I asked.

"You tell me," Buchan replied, an odd look on his face.

The creature in the trap was unlike anything I have ever seen, alive or dead. There seemed to be something of every animal in it, yet not enough of one to identify the whole. It had the teeth of a rodent, the claws of a lynx, a tail like an opossum's, the build of a fox, a snout like a bear's, and the wide, flat skull of a badger, with deep-set eyes that glowed bright red. Stranger than the creature being slat thin was it being completely devoid of fur. Its naked flesh was ashen and covered with suppurating sores, which stank like rotting meat. Judging from its smell and contorted position, it was clear to the naked eye that the animal was dead. Yet although its left foreleg was firmly clamped within the jaws of the cunningly concealed fox trap, I did not notice any signs of blood, either fresh or frozen, in the fresh layer of snow.

"Sweet mother of God—what is that thing?" I gasped.

"I'll be deviled if I know," Buchan replied, eyeing the wretched beast with open distaste. "Perhaps a freakish wolverine, or a raccoon eat-up with the mange. In any case, it's of no use to me or the Hudson Bay Company."

However, as Buchan moved to free the carcass from the trap, the supposedly dead animal miraculously came back to life and, with a vicious snarl, sank its yellowed fangs between the trapper's thumb and forefinger.

"*Son of a whore!*" Buchan bellowed. Without a moment's hesitation he pulled the skinning knife from his belt and plunged it into the foul beast's right eye, killing it once and for all.

"Are you alright, Dick?" I asked, staring at the bright red blood that now stained the white snow.

"I'm fine," he replied stoically, wrapping his wound with a length of cloth from his coat pocket. "It's not the first time I got bit by something I caught." He picked up the empty trap and slung it over his shoulder. "I'm going to move a hundred yards up the line, just in case there are any more like that bastard nosing about."

As I trudged after my friend, I glanced back at the strange creature, only to see its gaunt and hairless body sinking into the snow, as if the very land was conspiring to obliterate all traces of its existence.

After a breakfast of pemmican and black coffee, I shouldered my pack and, after bidding Buchan farewell and good hunting, headed east, dragging my sledge behind me. I quickly put the strange, hairless creature out of my mind. Obviously it was some kind of diseased freak of nature. What else could it have been? In any case, the beast's days had been numbered, even before it wandered into Buchan's trap. How much longer could it have continued to survive the winter?

I spent a fortnight in the wilderness along the line, checking, emptying, and resetting my traps, living off the land as well as my provisions, thanks to my trusty rifle. The work was hard and the weather unaccommodating, but nearly every night I enjoyed a meal of fricassee rabbit or roasted spruce grouse, and slept in comparative warmth and comfort. There are many who toil in the factories of Toronto and Winnipeg who cannot make such a claim.

As I arrived back at the home shanty, my sledge groaning under the weight of the early winter bounty, I saw was my other partner, Ben Martin, chopping wood in the dooryard. He had returned the day before with an impressive number of beaver and mink to his credit. That night we sat in front of the camp stove and exchanged tales of our foray into the bush while enjoying Jack's venison cutlets.

I related the tale of the strange, hairless beast Buchan caught, and we had a good laugh at our partner's expense. Rather, I should say Martin and I found it humorous, as the story seemed to unsettle Jack. As I turned in that night, I fully expected to see Buchan trudge into camp within the next day or so, cursing a blue streak, as was his habit, and bellowing for hot coffee and a plate of beans.

However, two days passed without Buchan's return. And then another. Come the evening of the fourth day, Martin and I decided to go looking for him. Buchan could have fallen victim to a bear or a mountain lion, perhaps even wolves. But he could have just as easily—and far more likely—run afoul of poachers, most of which would not think twice about killing an unwary trapper for his furs.

The next day we harnessed up the dogs and set out into the vast Manitoban wilderness, with Martin acting as musher and me riding in the sledge's basket, my rifle cocked and ready in case of trouble.

Thanks to the dogs, we reached the first tilt on the eastern spoke within an hour. Upon arrival, we were surprised to see what looked to be Buchan's sledge parked beside the shelter, buried underneath a heavy shroud of snow. Martin and I exchanged worried looks. Whatever fate had befallen our friend, it had happened shortly after his arrival, over two weeks ago.

I knelt down and lifted the hide that served as the makeshift door of the tilt, only to recoil from the smell that came from inside. I was instantly reminded of the diseased creature that had bitten Buchan, and I wondered—somewhat belatedly—if the beast might have suffered from leprosy or some other communicable illness. After my eyes adjusted from the bright glare of the snow to the dim interior of the shelter, I could make out a figure huddled on the floor, wrapped in filthy blankets.

"Buchan—is that you?" I asked warily, poking the lump with my rifle.

Whatever was inside the mass stirred feebly and issued a groan so anguished it set the hairs on the back of my neck on end. I put aside my gun and motioned for Martin to help me pull Buchan free of the tilt. As our friend emerged from the rank darkness, I was shocked to see his strapping frame reduced to little more than skin and bones. If not for his moaning and a feeble stirring of his limbs, I would have thought him dead.

"Merciful God, Buchan. What happened to you?" Martin exclaimed.

The best our partner could do by way of a response was to lift his right hand, which was swollen to three times its normal size and black with infection. It was from this putrid wound that the smell of rotting meat came. Buchan's eyes were sunken deep into his skull and seemed as capable of sight as billiard balls.

Martin and I wrapped him in the bear skin we had brought with us, but as we drew near the sled, the dogs began growling and barking, and a couple even lunged as if to attack. Martin had to take the whip to the wretched beasts, cursing them at the top of his lungs, in order to get them back in line.

I sat in the basket of the sled, holding Buchan tightly in my arms, while Martin drove the dogs. A mile or two out from our base camp, a snow storm started up. As it grew stronger I thought I heard something that sounded like wailing hidden within the wind. Buchan, who had lain as still as a dead man until this point, suddenly began to tremble and twitch, as if taken by a fit. I shouted to Martin to get us home as fast as possible.

By the time we reached the home shanty, the snowstorm had become a blizzard, blasting us with sleet that stung like millions of tiny icy knives. Jack hurried to greet us, only to halt upon catching sight of Buchan, whom we dragged between us as if escorting a drunken friend home from a bar. The look on the Cree's face was one of utter fear.

"Don't stand there gawking!" Martin snapped. "Get the dogs out of harness and feed them!"

Jack nodded his understanding and moved out of the way, giving us a wide berth. Martin and I entered the cabin, placing Buchan on his own bunk. As he lay there, I was struck by the peculiar sensation that what lay before me was not, in fact, the man I'd lived and worked alongside for the better part of a year, but an *approximation*. I instantly realized how absurd a fancy it was, yet I could not help but feel that someone—or *some thing*—had hollowed out Buchan and climbed inside, and was now looking out at me through stolen eyes.

Buchan's moaning became a groan and he began to writhe underneath his blankets, as if something was gnawing on him. His eyes opened and he licked his chapped and bleeding lips with a pinkish-gray tongue. It was clear from the look in his eyes that he wanted desperately to communicate something to us.

"What is it, Dick?" Martin asked, leaning close so as to hear.

Buchan's voice was as dry and brittle as kindling, but there was no mistaking what he said: *"Hungry...."*

"Rest easy, chum," Martin said reassuringly. "You're safe now. I'll have Jack fix you some soup."

This seemed to placate Buchan, and he lapsed back into unconsciousness. Martin took me aside and spoke in a low voice so he would not be overheard. He had been a barber-surgeon before coming to Manitoba, and as such served as the camp physician when necessary.

"He's got a raging fever," he said grimly. "He's got to lose that hand if he wants to survive, no question about it. But I'm going to need laudanum from the trading post if I'm to amputate."

"I'll go fetch it."

"Are you sure you want to risk it? That's a pretty bad storm out there, and it'll be getting dark soon...."

"Buchan would do the same for either of us," I replied. "Besides, the dogs know the way there and back by instinct, storm or no. You and Jack try to keep him alive while I'm gone."

"Speaking of which—where'd that red devil get off to?" Martin frowned. "It doesn't take *that* long to feed dogs."

I threw my parka back on and went outside, shouting for Jack to get the harness and gang lines back out. As I went behind the cabin to where the dogs were penned, I looked around for some sign of the camp cook, but he was nowhere to be found. Then I realized two things at the exact same time: the smaller of the two dogsleds was gone, and half the dogs were missing.

Martin was kneeling beside Buchan's cot, wrapping the ailing man's hand in bandages soaked in hot water in order to draw the infection out. He looked up at the sound of my cursing, which preceded my arrival by a good thirty seconds.

"That son of a bitch Jack has run off, and he's taken most of the dogs!"

"When this damned storm has blown over and Buchan is on the mend, I'm going to make it a point of tracking that heathen bastard down and skinning him like a beaver!" Martin growled.

"He was always an odd duck, if you ask me," I replied. "When he saw us carrying Buchan, you would have thought he'd seen the devil himself. Something scared him. I'll be damned if I know what."

I lost no time hitching up the three remaining dogs to what was now our only sled and striking out for the trading post, which was twenty-five miles from the camp. Normally it would take two-and-half hours to get there, but that was in good weather. With the storm as bad as it was, I had to trust in the dogs' instincts and sense of direction, as the trail that lead through the forest was all but obliterated by the wind.

After an hour or so, the storm suddenly dissipated and the dogs were able to pick up the pace. Just as the sun was about to set, I was rewarded by the sight of the fort-like walls of the God's Lake trading post. My team glided through the front gates just as they were preparing to close them for the night.

Inside the trading post were several buildings, including a kennel for visiting trappers to house their sled teams. I paid the old Indian who hobbled out to greet me a few shillings to feed and water my dogs. Taking the bundle of furs I'd brought with me from the sled, I then headed into the store to do my trading.

The interior of the Hudson Bay Company store was not that different from the average mercantile in Winnipeg. Inside the large log building a counter ran along the right side of the room, with a glass case on the end, displaying such items as horn-handled buck knives and six-shooters. The shelves along the wall behind the counter were stocked with bolts of cloth and other merchandise. Several items of clothing, such as flannel shirts and heavy jackets, hung from the ceiling. Opposite the counter, standing in the very middle of the room, was a large metal stove, about which were gathered several wooden chairs.

The clerk behind the counter was a dark-haired Welshman, whom I had had dealings with before and was friendly with. He lifted an eyebrow as I dropped my bundle of furs before him.

"You're here late," he commented as he sorted through what I'd brought him. "Will you be putting up for the night, then?"

"Not tonight," I replied with a shake of my head. "I've got to get back to camp. Buchan's down sick. Martin sent me in to trade for laudanum and rubbing alcohol. I also need a couple of dogs to replace some stolen from me."

"Buchan, eh? That's odd. The gentleman over there was just asking about him earlier."

"What gentleman?"

"The one warming himself by the stove."

I turned to look in the direction the clerk pointed, and spotted a figure sitting hunched in one of the chairs drawn close to the stove, puffing on a pipe. He was dressed all in black and sitting so still I had not noticed him when I first entered the room. At least, that is the only reason for why I could have overlooked such a distinctive individual.

Judging from the gray in his hair and mustache-less beard, the man was in his fifties, with a physique seasoned by sun and hard work. Indeed, his skin was tanned so deep a brown he looked to have been cast of bronze. As I dropped my gaze, I saw that his right leg was missing just below the knee, beneath which he wore an artificial one made of ivory.

Although unusual as his prosthesis might have been, it was nothing compared to his manner of dress, which was not only woefully inappropriate for the harsh climate of Manitoba, but also strangely anachronistic, seeming to be at least twenty-five years or more out of date. It consisted of a black wool mariner's jacket, a dark-colored cravat, and an odd-looking wide-brimmed black felt hat with a buckled ribbon band.

"Where did *he* come from?" I exclaimed. The sight of a sailor at the trading post was not that unusual, for the merchant marines aboard the ships that ferried the Hudson Bay Company's stockpile of furs to England often came ashore, but that was during the spring, after the thaw had melted the ice.

"I'll be damned if I know," the clerk replied with a shrug. "The old Indian who sees to the gate said he simply walked up out of the snow, just as you see him here. Mighty queer business all around, if you ask me, what with all those *thees* and *thous* of his."

As the clerk went about tallying up the furs I brought in for trade, I decided to see what this strange, solitary figure wanted with Buchan.

"Excuse me, mister—?"

As the sailor turned toward me, I realized my attention had been so focused on his peg-leg and clothes I had somehow failed to notice the slender, livid white scar that started in the hairline above his brow and ran down his face, disappearing behind the cravat knotted about his neck. Whether it was a birthmark or evidence of some horrific wounding, I could not tell.

The one-legged man glanced at my outstretched hand, but did not move to take it. Instead, he removed the pipe from his mouth and slightly bowed his head in acknowledgment. "I was once called captain," he intoned in a rich, deep voice. "But thou may call me Ahab."

"I'm told you've been looking for Dick Buchan."

"Aye, that I am, lad," Ahab said, nodding his head once again. "Dost thou know where I might find him?"

"He's one of my partners," I explained. "Are you a friend of his?"

Ahab shook his head as he returned the pipe to his mouth. "I have never met the gentleman. All the same, I have business of the utmost importance with him."

"Might I inquire as to the nature of that business?" I asked.

"My own," Ahab replied curtly. The dark look the older man gave me was enough to stop me from pressing the matter.

"I'm sorry if my question offended you, sir. Do you mind if I sit and warm myself?" I asked, pointing to the pot-bellied stove as I drew up a chair.

The man called Ahab nodded and silently gestured with his pipe for me to join him. As I sat beside him, I fought the desire to stare at the strange mark about the older man's neck, and instead focused my attention on the same thing as he: the glowing embers and flickering flames on view through the vents in the stove's hinged door.

After a couple of minutes I grew equal parts bored and bold and decided to resume my questioning. "I take it from your clothes that you are a sailor?"

Ahab nodded and said with a small, humorless laugh, "Though now I am dry-docked, I once spent forty of my fifty-three years at sea."

"Did your ship come into the Bay before it froze?"

The darkness that had previously filled Ahab's eyes now threatened to reappear. He shook his head and returned his gaze to the stove. "No—I came a different way."

"Do not take my question wrongly, sir; but your manner of speech is most unusual—where do you hail from?"

"I am a Nantucket Quaker, good sir," Ahab replied, not without a touch of pride. "A Yankee, if thee will."

"You are very far from home, then."

"Farther than thee can imagine," the old sailor said, his voice melancholy. He took the pipe from his mouth and gave it a sharp rap against his peg-leg, knocking the ashes onto the floor. "Enjoying a good smoke is one of the few solaces those such as me and thee—men who make our living on the knife-edge of the world—can count on," he said, waxing philosophical. "Yet once, in a fit of pique, I threw my pipe in the ocean because it could not soothe me. But now all is forgiven between us, and it provides me comfort once again."

I was about to ask Ahab how he could possibly be smoking the same pipe he had hurled into the sea, when the clerk called out that he'd finished his accounting. I excused myself from the old salt's company and returned to the counter.

"I can trade you the laudanum and rubbing alcohol, but not the dogs," the clerk said, pointing to the bottle of Dr. Rabbitfoot's Tincture of Opium.

"Can't you extend us credit? You know we're good for it. The dogs I got now aren't enough to last the winter. If one or two go lame or die on me, I'll be on foot until spring."

"I wish I could help you out, but the Company don't allow credit," the clerk said with a shrug of his shoulders. "Cash on the barrelhead or trade only—them's the rules."

A sun-darkened hand suddenly slapped down onto the clerk's open ledger, placing a gold coin atop the page.

"I'll buy thee the dogs thou needest, my friend," Ahab said. "Granted I ride with thee to thy camp."

The clerk picked up the gold piece and turned it over in his hands, giving out a low whistle of admiration. The coin was a doubloon, the border of which was stamped *Republica del Ecuador: Quito.* On the face were three mountains: on top the first was a flame, the second a tower, while atop the third was a crowing rooster. Above the three mountains was a portion of the zodiac, with the sun entering the equinox under the sign of Libra. The coin seemed to glow in the dim light of the trading post, as if it possessed a life of its own.

"What say thee, clerk?" Ahab said. "Is that coin enough to buy his dogs?"

"But there's a hole in the middle of it ..." the clerk pointed out weakly.

"It is *gold*, is it not?" Ahab said sternly, in a voice that could be heard through a hurricane. "Now give the man his dogs!"

The clerk cringed as if he'd been struck with a cat o' nine tails. "Yes, sir," he replied obsequiously. "As you wish, sir."

As the clerk wrapped the supplies I'd come for in a bundle of rags to protect them from breaking, I turned back to face the man called Ahab.

"I appreciate your generosity, sir. And you are welcome to ride with me back to our camp. But I warn you, Buchan is extremely ill. In fact, I came to the post to trade for medicine in hopes it will save his life. There is a very good chance that he will be dead by the time we get back."

"All the more important that we leave as soon as possible," Ahab said grimly.

As I headed for the door, the sea captain fell in step behind me. There was a line of pegs on the wall just inside the door, upon which were hung several different outer garments, including my own. As I pulled on my gear, I was surprised to see Ahab reach, not for a coat, but for a harpoon that stood propped up against the doorjamb.

It stood taller than the man himself, with a shaft fashioned from a hickory pole still bearing strips of bark. The socket of the harpoon was braided with the spread yarns of a towline, which lay coiled on the floor like a Hindoo fakir's rope. The lower end of the rope was drawn halfway along the pole's length, and tightly secured with woven twine, so that pole, iron, and rope remained inseparable. The harpoon's barb shone like a butcher's knife-edge in the dim light. It was indeed a fearsome weapon, made all the more intimidating by its incongruity.

"Where is your coat, sir?" I exclaimed, when I realized that my new companion planned to step outside dressed exactly as he was. "It's below freezing outside!"

"Do not concern thyself for my comfort," Ahab said calmly. "I have been in far more inhospitable climes of late."

"Why do you carry a harpoon on dry land?" I asked, shaking my head in disbelief.

"Where a shepherd has his crook, and the cowboy his lariat, this is the instrument of my profession," the old mariner said matter-of-factly. "Wherever I go, it follows with me."

As we approached the kennel to fetch my team, the dogs set up an awful racket. However, it was not the snarling expected from sled dogs jockeying amongst themselves for dominance within the pack, but growling born of genuine fear. The lead dog, his nape bristling and ears flat against his skull, snapped at me as I moved to harness him. If I had not jerked my hand back when I did, I most certainly would have lost some fingers.

Before I could unfurl my dog-whip, Ahab stepped forward and planted the butt of the harpoon in the frozen mud of the kennel yard, glowering at the wildly barking huskies with those strange eyes of his. One by one, the dogs fell silent and lowered their heads, skulking away, tails tucked between their legs, without the old sea captain having to utter a single word.

"How did you do that?" I asked, amazed by what I had just seen.

"I have stared down my share of mutineers in my day," Ahab replied. "There is not much difference between a dog and a deckhand; if they smell the slightest whiff of fear, they will tear thee limb from limb."

I added the three new dogs Ahab had staked me to my existing team and harnessed them to my sled. I served as musher, while Ahab sat in the basket. With an old horse blanket draped about his shoulders for warmth, and his harpoon held across his lap, the dour sea captain looked like some grim Norse king preparing for his final battle.

As we exited through the trading post's gates, I looked up at the night sky to find it filled with the shifting radiance of the Aurora Borealis. It was by this light that we made our way back to camp.

Once we were off, Ahab did not utter a single word, but instead stared into the darkness, lost in whatever thoughts he kept locked inside his head. As a man who turned his back on the predictability of city life in favor of a wilderness as isolated and unknown as the uncharted ocean, I felt a certain kinship toward the taciturn Quaker who had forsaken the certainty of solid ground for a pitching deck and the vast horizon of the open sea, despite his strange demeanor.

The weather for the return trip was cold but otherwise clear until a mile or so out from our destination. Suddenly the wind picked up and quickly grew to gale-force, accompanied by increasing snowfall. Once more, I heard the eerie wailing within the storm, which grew stronger the closer we got. I could not escape the sensation that somehow the blizzard sensed our approach, and was not at all pleased by the intrusion.

The snow was so heavy I could barely discern the outline of the cabin. Despite my heavy boots and fur-lined gloves, my hands and feet felt like blocks of ice. I was looking forward to warming myself by the fireplace, the humble chimney of which jutted from the roof of the shanty like the bowl of a giant's pipe. Given my own chilliness, I could only imagine the discomfort Ahab was experiencing. He'd said that he'd lost one leg to a whale, which I had no reason to doubt, and now I feared he might lose the other to frostbite, as well as some fingers. My concern proved to be ill placed, however, for he climbed out of the basket as easily as if he was stepping out of a carriage. Using his harpoon as a walking stick, Ahab made his way toward the darkened cabin without so much as a backward glance.

"Come back here!" I shouted over the howling wind. "I need help putting up the dogs!"

If the sailor heard me, he made no show of it, but continued his beeline to the front door. I grabbed the lantern from the sled and hurried after him, cursing loudly the whole way. I knew Martin well enough to easily envision what his first reaction would be to the sight of an unannounced stranger armed with what looked like a spear entering his abode in the middle of the night. I caught up with the Quaker before he could put his shoulder to the door.

"Are you daft?" I growled. "If you go barging into a trapper's cabin like that, you're apt to get shot for an Indian or a poacher! And I am in no hurry to clean your brains off my walls!"

"Forgive me, friend," Ahab said, stepping aside so I might go ahead of him. "The prospect of concluding my business has made me ... incautious."

Holding up the lantern so that its light would illuminate my face as well as the darkness, I pushed open the door of the shanty. The interior of the cabin was as dark as a well digger's snuffbox.

"Martin! Hold your fire and sheath your knife! It's me!" I called out. "And I have brought a visitor."

I expected to hear my partner's voice in return, telling me to close the damned door before I let in a polar bear, but there was no reply. I crossed the threshold into the darkness, Ahab's ivory peg-leg tapping against the rough-hewn planks of the cabin floor close behind.

I hadn't taken more than a couple of steps before I collided with a piece of furniture. I lowered the lantern so I could see where I was going and was shocked to find the interior of the cabin in utter chaos. The table on which my companions and I ate our meals had been reduced to kindling, along with its accompanying chairs, as if demolished in a brawl. My heart sank at the sight of several sacks of flour and sugar—provisions for the entire winter—dumped amidst scattered traps, furs, cookware, and clothes. The fire in the stone hearth had gone out, its ashes kicked out into the middle of the room, and the cabin was nearly as cold as the wilderness beyond its walls.

"Martin! Buchan! Where are you?" I cried, swinging the lantern about in hopes of it illuminating some sign of my friends. My mind rushed about in circles, as if caught in one of my traps. Had poachers broken into the cabin, looking for furs to steal? Or was this the result of an Indian attack? Perhaps Jack had returned, and he and Martin got into a fight?

I fell silent, hoping I might detect a response. Instead, all I heard was a low, grunting noise, like that of a rooting hog, coming from the back of the cabin, where the shadows were the darkest. Lifting high the lantern, I moved to investigate the sound.

I found Buchan—or rather, what had become of him—crouching in the corner. His back was turned toward me and I could see not only that he was completely naked, but every vertebrae along his spine as well.

"Buchan—what happened? Where's Martin?"

In response, Buchan spun around to face me, growling like a cornered dog. Save that he was covered in skin, which was by now ash-gray and fairly bursting with weeping sores, he was little more than a skeleton. He was so gaunt the ribs in his chest stood out like the staves of barrel, and his diseased flesh was pulled so tautly across his pelvis it looked as if it was wrapped in leather. But the worst of it was that Buchan's face was smeared with gore and saliva, and in his bony, claw-like hands he clutched the half-devoured remains of a raw liver. I was so shocked by his wretched condition, I did not at first realize that Martin lay sprawled at Buchan's feet, split open from anus to throat, his guts scooped out and piled beside him like those of a field-dressed deer.

Suddenly, strong, iron-hard fingers dug into my shoulder. It was Ahab. I had been so horrified I had forgotten he was there.

"Stand aside, friend," the sea captain said grimly. "For this is the business I must attend to." Ahab hoisted the harpoon, his voice booming in the close confines of the cabin like ocean waves breaking against the shore. "*Wendigo! Cannibal Spirit of the North! I am Ahab, hunter of fiends! And in the Devil's name, I have come to claim you!*"

I do not know if the light from the lantern held in my trembling hand played tricks on me, or if what I saw was what indeed happened; but as Ahab hurled the harpoon, the thing I knew as Dick Buchan seemed to grow, like a shadow cast upon a wall, becoming taller and even thinner than before. He then turned sideways, seeming to disappear, causing the razor-sharp harpoon to sail past harmlessly and imbed itself into the wall of the cabin.

Buchan reappeared just as suddenly as he had disappeared, but now he was standing in front of the hearth of the fireplace. With a terrible shriek, more like that of a wounded elk than a man, he raised his arms above his head, causing his body to elongate yet again, and shot straight up the fireplace chimney. I was so dumbfounded I at first did not believe my own eyes—until I heard the sound of footsteps on the roof overhead, followed by a wild, maniacal laughter.

Ahab snatched the harpoon free and hurried for the door, moving as fast as his missing leg allowed. He charged out into the snowstorm, bellowing curses in seven different languages with the heedless bravery peculiar to those who have hunted down and slain creatures a thousand times their size. The dogs—still in harness and attached to their gang line—frantically barked at whatever it was that was stamping back and forth across the roof over their heads.

As I crossed the threshold to join my companion, I felt something snag the hood of my parka. I looked up and, to my horror, saw a long, bony arm reaching down from the eaves above. I tried to tear myself free of whatever had hold of me, but was unable to break its grip. The thing on the roof gave a single tug, as if testing the strength of its hold, and I found that my boots no longer touched the ground.

As I was dragged upwards to whatever awaited me on the roof, my mind flashed back to Martin's fate, and I began to kick and scream as hard as I could. Suddenly Ahab was there beside me, jabbing at the thing on the roof with his harpoon.

"Leave him be, wendigo!" he shouted angrily. "Thou hast feasted enough for one night!"

The creature cried out in pain and released its hold, sending me tumbling into a snowdrift. As I got to my feet I saw it squatting on the roof like a living gargoyle. It no longer bore any resemblance to Buchan, save that it was roughly the shape of a man. Its arms and legs were as long as barge poles, and the horns of an elk grew from its skull. Its eyes were pushed so far back in their orbits they at first seemed to be missing—until I caught a flicker of reddish light in each socket, like those of a wild animal skulking beyond a campfire. Its lips were tattered and peeled back from its gums, revealing long, curving tusks the color of ivory. Even from where I stood, I could smell its stink—that of death and decay, just like the horrid freak that had bitten poor Buchan.

"Laugh all thee like, monster!" Ahab shouted at the ghastly apparition. "Thou shalt not escape! I did not drown thirty good men to be bested by the likes of thee!"

As if in reply, the creature shrieked like a wild cat, its voice melding with the whistling north wind. It got to its feet and jumped from the roof of the cabin to a nearby pine tree, clearing a distance of thirty feet as easily as a child playing hop-scotch. As I watched in amazement, the creature darted to the very top of the towering pine, which swayed wildly back and forth in the wind, climbing with the agility of an ape.

Ahab drew back his arm and hurled his harpoon at the abomination a second time. It shot forth as if fired from a cannon, the towline flapping behind it like a pennant, only to fall short of its target. Apparently unfazed, the beast leapt into the uppermost crown of the tree beside it, and then the one after that. Within seconds it had disappeared from sight, its scream of triumph fading into the distance.

"Come inside," I said. "The thing is gone. It's over."

Ahab shook his head in disgust as he trudged back into the cabin, his harpoon slung over one shoulder like a Viking's spear. "It will not wander far—not while there is still meat on our bones."

I did not argue with the man, but instead busied myself with releasing the dogs from their gang line. As I returned them to the kennel, I decided it would be wise to keep them in their harnesses, as I foresaw a need to leave camp in a hurry.

Upon returning inside the cabin, I found a fire set in the hearth and saw that Ahab had draped a length of canvas over Martin's savaged corpse. The old sailor sat on a stool that was still in one piece in front of the fireplace, sharpening his harpoon with a piece of whetstone.

"You owe me an explanation, old man," I said sternly. "Whatever your business with Buchan, it now concerns me."

"Fair enough," Ahab replied. "Ask me what thou wilt, and I will answer thee true. But I warn thee, friend—thou might find this truth unbecoming to reason."

"You seem to know what that thing is—you called it *wendigo*. What is it?"

"It is a spirit, of sorts. The Indians of the North—the Cree, the Inuit, the Ojibwa—know it well," he explained, pausing to light his pipe. "It comes with the winter storms and is driven by a horrible hunger for human flesh. Some say it overtakes those who stay too long alone in the wilderness, while others claim it possesses only those driven to cannibalism. Of the last I have my doubts, for I have known many a cannibal in my travels, some of whom were men of good character, if not Christian disposition."

I stared at Ahab for a long moment, trying to determine if he truly believed what he had just told me. Under normal circumstances I would have laughed and called him a lunatic. But things were far from normal, as evidenced by poor Martin, lying there under his makeshift shroud.

"How is it you knew poor Buchan was afflicted by the wendigo?"

"My friend, are thee sure of thine desire for knowledge?" Seeing the steadfast-ness in my gaze, the old sailor gave a heavy sigh. "Very well, I shall answer thee, as promised. It is my business to know the unknowable, for I have been set a task unlike any since the labors of Hercules. Where once I hunted the great beasts of the ocean, now I stalk the fiends of Hell."

I could no longer hide my incredulity, and responded to this declaration with a rude laugh. "Have you lost your mind?"

"I was once mad, but no more," Ahab said sadly. "Would that I had the balm of insanity to allay my suffering; for I am just as sane as thee, my friend, if infi-nitely more damned."

"What are you babbling about?" I snapped, my patience finally worn thin.

"Once, decades ago, I bragged of being immortal on land and on sea. Now I find I must bear the burden of that boast for all eternity."

As I listened to the old sailor's rant, the hairs on my neck stood erect. The dark fire deep in Ahab's eyes frightened me in a way the wendigo's did not. It was one thing to be stalked by a fiendish creature, quite another to be trapped with a lunatic.

"Ah, I see the look in thine eyes," Ahab said with a grim smile. "Thou hadst seen what thou hath seen, and yet thee still deem me mad? What of *this*, then?" He pulled aside the cravat about his throat, revealing the marks of a noose no man could have survived. "Aye, I am dead. I have been such since long before your birth. I was once a righteous, God-fearing man, but I was made wicked by my pride and blasphemous by my wrath. I was determined to avenge myself on the whale that took my leg, and offered up my immortal soul in exchange for its annihilation.

"It did not matter to me that I had a child-bride and an infant son awaiting me in Nantucket. Nor did it matter that thirty men, brave and true, had placed their lives and livelihoods in my care. There was a fire in my bosom that burned day and night, and naught would extinguish it, save the blood of the whale that maimed me. Now my child-bride is a withered crone, my infant son dead on the end of a Confederate's bayonet, and my brave crew, save for one, sleeps at the bottom of the sea.

"I chased the accursed beast halfway across the world, and sank my harpoon into its damned hide, only to run afoul of the line. A flying turn of rope wrapped itself about my neck, yanking me below the waves, drowning me within seconds. Yet, to my horror, though I knew myself dead, I was still aware of all that transpired about me. I was helpless witness to the destruction of my ship and the deaths of my men by the whale I had pursued across three seas and two oceans.

"And when it was over, the hated whale pulled me down, down, down—past sunken galleons, past the lairs of slumbering leviathans, past the drowned towers of long-lost kingdoms—down to the very floor of the ocean. With dead man's eyes I beheld a great chasm, from which boiled dreadful beasts with the bodies of men and heads like that of jellyfish. These abominations freed me of my tether and escorted me down into the rift, which lead into the very belly of the world, Hell itself. There I swam not through a mere lake of fire, but an entire ocean, until I came at last to a great throne.

"The throne was fashioned of horn and upon it sat the King of the Fallen, the Devil himself. The Lord of the Damned resembled nothing so much as a gigantic shadow in the shape of a man, with wings of flame and eyes that shone like burnished shields. The Devil spoke unto me, and though he had no mouth, his voice rang like a gong, shaking me to my marrow.

"'Ahab,' he said, 'Thou promised me thine soul in exchange for the life of the whale. Yet here you stand before me, and the fish still swims! Let it not be said that I do not honor my covenants. I have within my kingdom a park unlike any seen on Earth, with trees of bone and rivers of blood. I would populate it with monsters for the pleasure of my sport. Bring me as many fiends as men you led to death, and I shall return thy soul, to do with as thou wish.'"

Although I did not want to believe the outrageous tale the old sailor had just told me, my curiosity got the better of me. "How many men died under your command?"

"Nine and twenty," he replied solemnly.

"And how many monsters have you hunted?"

"This will be the second," he admitted. "There. I have told thee what thou asked, nothing more, nothing less. I have come to this place on the Devil's business, and I cannot leave until it is finished. It is as simple as that."

"I have had enough of this lunacy!" I exclaimed, hoping the anger in my voice would hide the fear in my heart. "You are welcome to the cabin, but I am taking the dogs and returning to the trading post!"

"The wendigo will be upon thee within minutes of setting forth," Ahab cautioned.

"I have my rifle and my axe," I countered. "I won't be as easy to kill as Martin."

"Mortal weapons are of no use against that thing."

"It seemed to let go of me quickly enough when you jabbed it with that over-glorified pig-sticker of yours," I pointed out.

"This is no mere harpoon," Ahab said, nodding to the spear lying across his lap. "It was forged from the hardest iron there is: the nail-stubs of steel horse-shoes—the ones that racehorses wear. I myself hammered together the twelve rods for its shank, winding them together like the yarns of a rope. The barbs were cast from my own shaving razors—the finest, sharpest steel to ever touch human skin. But, most important of all, it was tempered not in water, but the blood of three pagan hunters, who, at my bidding, opened their veins so that the instrument of my revenge might partake of their strength. Thus I baptized it not in the name of the Father, but the Devil himself. *That* is why the wendigo feared it."

"All that may very well be true, but I am not a man prone to fancy. If I can see a thing, and hear a thing, and most certainly *smell* a thing, then to my mind it is of this world, not the next. And that means I can *kill* it. And if it gets in my way, I will do just that, Devil's menagerie or no!"

"I have no claim on thee," Ahab said quietly as he returned to his whetstone. "Escape if thee can."

I had no idea if Ahab was mad, damned, or a liar, and I had no desire to find which was the truth. Lantern in hand, I left the cabin and hurried to the pen where the dogs were kept. However, before I was halfway there I heard an unholy cacophony of yelps and barks. I quickened my pace, trying not to lose my footing in the knee-high snow and ice, and arrived at the dog-pen just in time to see the wendigo attack the last of the team.

The wendigo, now easily twice the size of man, held the hapless animal by the tail and lowered it, head-first, into its gaping mouth, the jaws of which were dislocated like those of a serpent. The fiend's belly was hideously dis-tended, far beyond human limits, and I could clearly see the outlines of the other dogs squirming underneath its ash-gray skin as they were digested alive. The wendigo's jaws snapped shut like a trap, severing the tail of the last dog, which fell to the snow in a gout of crimson.

I had been so horrified by the scene before me, I was rooted to the spot. But the sight of the dog's blood snapped me out of my petrified state, and I turned and fled back to the safety of the cabin. I did not dare turn and look behind me, for fear of what I might see in pursuit.

As I burst into the cabin, I found Ahab where I had left him, patiently applying the whetstone to his harpoon. "The dogs are dead!" I shouted. "It ate all of them!"

Ahab nodded as if this was something to be expected. "The wendigo is hunger incarnate. No matter how much it eats, its belly is never full; it exists in a perpetual state of starvation. The more it eats, the larger it grows; the larger it grows, the hungrier it gets. There is no end to it."

My mind was still reeling from the fresh horror I had just witnessed, and was only just realizing I was trapped. While I might have been able to flee the wendigo using the sled, there was no way I could possibly escape the camp on foot. It was then I surrendered my disbelief and embraced Ahab's reality as my own.

"How can we fight against this monster?"

If Ahab had an answer I did not hear it, for, at that exact moment, the window in front of which I stood abruptly shattered inward. I turned to see an emaciated arm as long as I am tall reach through the broken sash. I screamed in terror as the wendigo's fingers, the tips black from frostbite, closed about my leg, dragging me inexorably toward whatever stood on the other side.

Ahab was on his feet as quick as lightning, his harpoon at the ready. Without hesitation he dashed forward and plunged the spear into the wendigo's arm. The monster screamed in agony and anger as it let go of me, the absurdly long extremity withdrawing like a snake fleeing a fire.

"I have cost it an arm, if I'm lucky!" the old sailor said excitedly, pointing to a foul-smelling, tar-like substance splashed across the floor. "That bastard won't escape me by climbing the rigging *this* time!"

Harpoon in hand, Ahab rushed out of the cabin and into the snowy night. I followed close behind, for fear the creature might return while he was gone. I saw Ahab standing in the door-yard beside the sled that was to have been my escape, surveying his surroundings with eyes accustomed to scanning the open ocean for the fleeting flash of a fluke or the spume of a distant whale.

"Thar she blows!" Ahab sang out, pointing to a shambling shape moving off in the distance. I could barely make out the gray silhouette framed against the darkness, but it was obvious that the wendigo's right arm hung uselessly at its side.

Ahab hurled his harpoon after the fleeing figure. Because it had its back to us, the creature was unable to play its trick of turning sideways and disappearing, and this time the harpoon found its target, striking the creature between the shoulder blades.

The wendigo roared in angry pain and instantly took flight, running faster than any creature on two legs ever could. Ahab quickly grabbed the towline attached to the end of the harpoon and secured it to the brush bow of the sled.

"Fare thee well, friend," Ahab said as he took his place behind the handlebars. "Lord willing, we shall never meet again, in this world or the next!" And with that the sled sped away, shooting across the snow-covered landscape like a longboat dragged by a stricken whale.

As the Devil's huntsman and his monstrous quarry disappeared from sight, I could hear Ahab's shouted curses carried on the wind, mixed with the unholy wail of the wendigo, until they became one and the same.

So exhausted was I by the terrors I had undergone, I returned to the cabin, where I immediately collapsed into a deep sleep. When I awoke the next day, it was to find the blizzard abated and a gun in my face.

I discovered that a posse had been sent out from the trading post in search of me on account of my stealing three dogs. I insisted that I was innocent of the charges—that the dogs had been paid for, cash on the barrelhead. But even if they had been willing to believe me in regard to the dogs, there was still the matter of the mutilated corpse that lay twenty feet from where I slept.

I was promptly arrested for the murder of Ben Martin—as well as Dick Buchan, even though his body was never found—and taken back to the trading post and locked up in the stockade. And here I sit, awaiting the thaw, when I will be taken down to Winnipeg and put on trial.

I tried to explain about Ahab, and how he had bought the dogs for me, but the clerk who had waited on me and took the doubloon in payment claims no such person was ever in his store, nor is there any coin in the trading post's coffers matching the description I gave.

My only hope is that Jack will reappear and vouch for what he saw in Buchan's gaunt, sunken eyes. For now, too late, I realize the reason for the Indian abandoning the camp. If he does not come forward, then I will either be hung as a murderer or imprisoned as a madman.

Sometimes, late at night, when the frigid wind blows out of the north and whistles cruelly through the bars of my cell, I still hear Ahab's voice as he is dragged across the vast, uncharted wilderness by his captured fiend: *"Run! Run! Run to thy infernal master! To the last I grapple with thee; from Hell's heart, I stab at thee!"*

Author Comments

Nancy Collins

"When I was in the second grade, I was taken to see John Huston's classic film adaptation of *Moby-Dick*, the one with Gregory Peck as Ahab. It made an immense impact on me—to the point I wanted to become a whaler when I grew up. I quickly outgrew the desire to hunt sea mammals, but I have always found Captain Ahab to be a compelling character, and one it would not be hard to imagine condemned to the same supernatural fate as Coleridge's Ancient Mariner."

Nancy Collins is currently working on the third installment of her new *Golgotham* urban-fantasy series. The second book in the series, *Left Hand Magic*, is scheduled for a December 2011 release by Penguin/Roc.

Joe R. Lansdale

"I wrote 'Dread Island' based on my love for Mark Twain, which collided with my interest in Lovecraft, and the fact that the Uncle Remus tales may have been the first stories I ever read. And then there were comics. I always saw 'Dread Island' as a kind of comic book in prose, the old Classics Illustrated look. That's how it played out in my head."

Joe R. Lansdale is the author of numerous novels and short stories, one of which is "Bubba Hotep," source of the cult film of the same name. His current novel is *Devil Red*.

Mike Resnick

"I wanted to do something totally off the wall, a funny Heinrich Himmler certainly fills the bill. He had to be opposed by Good Guys that most readers would know. The best-known woman of the 1940s was Eleanor Roosevelt, always dignified, always dressed to the hilt—so I saw her as a half-naked warrior princess. And I absolutely loved the notion of Albert Einstein, Master Sorcerer, chanting mathematical formulas instead of spells. I hope the readers have half as much fun reading it as I had writing it."

Mike Resnick is, according to *Locus* magaazine, the all-time leading award winner, living or dead, for short science fiction. He has won five Hugos (from a record 35 nominations), a Nebula, and other major and minor awards in the USA, Spain, Japan, Poland, Croatia, and France. He is the author of 60+ novels, 250+ short stories, and two screenplays, and is the editor of 40+ anthologies. His most recent books are *Blasphemy* and *The Buntline Special*; coming later this year are *The Doctor and The Kid* and *The Incarceration of Captain Nebula And Other Stories.* He has been named the Guest of Honor at the 2012 World Science Fiction Convention.

John Shirley

"I've always been drawn to the old west—and to horror. I did considerable research about Billy the Kid, and there were in fact rumors of his having survived into the 20th Century. But what most inspired the story were the famously-bad low-budget films *Billy the Kid Versus Dracula* and *Jesse James Meets Frankenstein's Daughter*, made back-to-back in 1966 by the prolific "One Shot William" Beaudine. It just seemed to me that placing Billy the Kid in the midst of that low-rent film setting was fraught with fun ... especially if we involved a "Victor Frankenstein" and Frankensteinian horror. The convergence of these curious elements took me into a nice fusion of drama, horror and humor."

John Shirley's newest novel release is *Bleak History* from Pocket Books; his new story collection is *In Extremis* from Underland Press, and eReads is re-releasing eleven of his books, including *Wetbones* and *The Other End*. He has two forthcoming: *Bioshock: Rapture* from Tor, and *Everything Is Broken* from Prime Books.

Rio Youers

"So I had this idea—a spark, really: a mash-up of Jim Morrison and Edgar Allan Poe, two American icons with esoteric tendencies. Naturally, I wanted to see what would happen, so I let concept dance in my mind … and before long had the story's blueprint. In writing, I found the elements (the darkness) melded seamlessly—an exciting, organic process fueled by my passion for the subjects' work."

Rio Youers was recently nominated for a British Fantasy Award for his novella *Old Man Scratch*. He has just completed his new novel, *In Faith*, and his short story collection, *Dark Dreams, Pale Horses* will be released by PS Publishing in early 2011.

Editor Comment

Jeff Conner

"Monster Lit is the industry term for the recent wave of fad-driven mash-up fiction that swept the publishing houses like a tsunami. This series of 3R books is designed as a corrective to the shallow, self-limiting formula of splicing public domain classics and/or historical icons with trendy genre elements. (You may have noticed that we are a zombie and vampire free zone.) We dig mashups and believe that there is far more potential in them than generic Monster Lit allows, so we call our brand CTL-ALT-LIT, as it better reflects our digital age and the remix culture we live in. Please enjoy responsibly."

Jeff Conner is a World Fantasy Award recipient who currently heads up IDW's line of original prose projects. Along with the three volumes of *RRR*, he recently worked on *GI JOE: Tales From The Cobra Wars*, a collection of original fiction set in the same world as IDW's *G.I. JOE* comics.